THE PERFECT STRANGER

Rosalind had never seen this dazzlingly handsome man before. But he had seen her.

"I've wanted to do this since the moment I saw you sitting here, all alone, like a pale green nymph escaped from the woods," he murmured.

At first his mouth felt soft, like the touch of a butterfly against her cheek. But as it trailed slowly toward her lips it left a path of heat that quickly turned to flame as it reached its destination.

At this perilous point, Rosalind realized she should break away, for she could hear already what wagging tongues would say. But drowning all that out was what her wildly beating heart was telling her. . . .

IRENE SAUNDERS, a native of Yorkshire, England, worked a number of years for the U.S. Air Force in London. A love of travel brought her to New York City, where she met her husband, Ray. She now lives in Port St. Lucie, Florida, dividing her time between writing, bookkeeping, gardening, needlepoint, and travel.

The Difficult Daughter

Irene Saunders

A SIGNET BOOK

SIGNET
Published by the Penguin Group
Penguin Books USA Inc., 375 Hudson Street,
New York, New York, 10014, U.S.A.
Penguin Books Ltd, 27 Wrights Lane, London W8 5TZ, England
Penguin Books Australia Ltd, Ringwood, Victoria, Australia
Penguin Books Canada Ltd, 10 Alcorn Avenue, Toronto, Ontario, Canada M4V 3B2
Penguin Books (N.Z.) Ltd, 182-190 Wairau Road,
Auckland 10, New Zealand

Penguin Books Ltd, Registered Offices:
Harmondsworth, Middlesex, England

First published by Signet, an imprint of New American Library,
a division of Penguin Books USA Inc.

First Printing, February, 1992

10 9 8 7 6 5 4 3 2 1

Chapter One

The fifth day of January in the year 1814 was a day long to be remembered by most of the inhabitants of the small county of Rutland. They would doubtless speak of it for the rest of their lives, and pass down to future generations much embellished accounts of the events, and of the parts each person had played in them.

The occasion was the christening, at Belvoir Castle, of the little Marquess of Granby, infant son and heir of the Fifth Duke of Rutland.

For more than a week there had been the keenest speculations as to whether this important event might have to be indefinitely postponed. Some had even gone so far as to declare a delay of even one day an ill omen, but there was naught else could be done, for a most dreadful fog had descended upon London and many miles beyond. It had brought all London to a standstill for the entire last week of 1813 and three days into the new year, delaying services and causing countless accidents.

But at last word came that the fog had lifted, and that the godfathers, none other than the Prince Regent himself, and his brother the Duke of York, were on their way. No less than three hundred of the county's gentry and yeomanry, led by Geoffrey Marshall, 3rd Viscount Stockton, made preparations to meet them and escort them to the castle.

"Must you go, my dear? Cannot Peter take your place this once, for January weather is always treacherous?" Lady Stockton plaintively asked her husband on realizing that her earlier exhortations had been completely disregarded. "You know that the duke would not wish you to come down with an inflammation of the lungs again, as you did but a twelve month ago."

The viscount smiled. He was seated behind the desk in his study, meticulously going over a list of things that must be done that day on the estates. He was a careful man, and wrote instructions to his bailiff about each and every one of them.

"Now Margaret, my love, do be sensible," he said gently. "What would happen if every man who agreed to take part were to suddenly decide, at the last minute, that the weather was too inclement for him? Rutland is relying upon me to keep some of the younger lads in order, and I'd not think to let him down. Peter is coming with me to give me a hand where necessary, but there is no question whatsoever of our son taking my place. I'm not yet in my dotage, you know."

"I'm well aware that you're not, but what will you do if it starts to rain, or even snow?" his lady asked, determined not to let him leave without a final protest.

"One thing we will not do is call upon our womenfolk to come dig us out," he said sharply, now becoming more than a little irritated by her persistence. "Just make sure that you and the girls have some warm wraps with you, though, or you'll be the ones who take ill. Peter and I will probably join you shortly before the banquet begins."

With a deep sigh, Lady Stockton went off to confer with Cook and make sure that a hearty breakfast awaited the two gentlemen. Then, after partaking of a meager portion herself and sipping her second cup of tea of the day with her menfolk, she went up the stairs once more to satisfy herself that her two younger daughters were already up and about. They should be, for a light breakfast had already been sent up to their bedchambers.

It would have been such a comfort if her oldest daughter could have been present today, but Patricia had met the most delightful young baron during her very first Season, married him a few months later, and was now in a most interesting condition, with a happy event expected very shortly. In the mind of Lady Stockton there was no doubt whatsoever that it would be a son, for Patricia had always behaved exactly as a young lady should, and had never for a moment caused them the slightest misgivings.

If only her second daughter, Rosalind, had done only half as well, she would now have been the happiest of mothers.

After tapping lightly on a bedchamber door, she entered at once and found that Rosalind was already dressed in the gown they had decided upon the day before, a quite simple pale green jaconet that looked particularly well with her shining chestnut curls. A matching green ribbon had been twisted through them to further accentuate their glow.

Eyeing her daughter critically, Lady Stockton had to admit to herself that Rosalind was by far the prettiest of her three daughters. If only she could be a little more tactful, a little less straightforward, she thought, she would have every young man in London at her feet.

"I've been trying to prevail upon your dear papa not to take part in the escort," Lady Stockton said distractedly, "but I might just as well have held my tongue for the good it did. It's high time that he left such things for Peter and the other younger men, for he's just asking for another month in bed, as he was last year.

"Just let me take a closer look at you to make sure that gown is really suitable. At least you've not worn it since we were in town last Season, and it's simple enough for few to realize they have seen it before."

Rosalind dutifully turned around so that her mama could see the whole of it, then she dropped her a low, graceful curtsy.

"Dear Mama," she said softly, "do stop worrying about Papa for he's been particularly well these last few months, and it's not as though Peter won't be there to keep an eye upon him. He'd not miss such a grand occasion as this for anything, and well you know it. Now, do you think I will be a credit to you?''

Lady Stockton nodded approvingly. "You'll do very nicely, if I do say so, but don't you have a green fan to match that gown? I always feel that a fan quite completes a gown, and can convey so much more than words when used correctly.''

Rosalind sighed, for this was one of her mama's pet projects. "If you recall, Mama, the only use I ever found for a fan was to rap Lord Butterworth's knuckles when he was in his cups and became a little too forward. It's just not my way to flutter my eyelashes at gentleman over the top of a fan, though there are many of my acquaintances who do it to great effect. I'd feel not only foolish but decidedly embarrassed were I to even try such a thing.''

Lady Stockton looked quite cross. "You should try what I see young Judith doing already,'' she admonished. "Practice in front of a mirror first until you can handle a fan charmingly without even thinking about it. And, speaking of Judith, I wonder what she can be doing all this time, for she started to dress a half hour before you did. Would you run across the hall, my dear, and find out what can be delaying her, while I make sure your papa does not need me again before he leaves?''

Rosalind was halfway there before her mama had finished speaking, and a moment later entered her sister's bedchamber only to find that young lady pulling off the gown her mama had selected, then dropping it on the floor and glaring at it in complete disgust. Their abigail, Hetty, looked harried.

"What's amiss with it?'' Rosalind asked, trying to hide a smile.

"Everything,'' Judith snapped. "My very first opportunity to be seen among London society and I have to wear an old thing like that. It makes me look like a little girl.''

Rosalind sighed. Judith was not yet seventeen, but she could scarcely bear to wait another year before having her come-out. "Why don't we ask Hetty to get that white sprigged gown I wore only a couple of times last Season, and I'll go and tell

Mama that your old one seems to be a little too tight for you?" she suggested.

"You'd not be telling stories, Miss Rosalind, for she's filled out some and it was tight on her. I'll just run and get yours," Hetty said, and they both hurried from the chamber.

Lady Stockton looked a little dubious when Rosalind informed her of the problem and its solution. But when a radiant Judith came down the stairs, not fifteen minutes later, she had to admit that Rosalind's gown looked most becoming on the child, and did not make her seem at all older than she was, though that had undoubtedly been Judith's objective.

Hot bricks had been placed in the carriage, although it was, in fact, an unusually mild day for early January, but the ladies were still glad of the warm wraps with which they had covered their finery.

Before the carriage had reached Belvoir Castle, however, both girls were tired of hearing Lady Stockton still grumbling that their papa was not here to escort them, though they should have been used to it, for such complaining was not at all rare for their mama. It seemed to Rosalind, however, that once a female married she ceased being a person in her own right, but became merely an appendage to her husband, and missed him quite dreadfully when his support was withdrawn for even the briefest of periods.

She stepped out of the carriage and followed her mama into the castle, recalling how, until its renovation was completed a year ago, it had resembled a seventeenth-century mansion rather than the castle it was named for. The present duke had ordered its transformation into something more befitting its name when his new bride had indicated her disappointment in what was to be her new home.

No sooner had Lady Stockton and her girls made their curtsies to the duke and duchess than the blare of horns heralded the arrival of the Prince Regent and his brother, the Duke of York.

Then came the sound of a twenty-one gun salute to the royal princes, and the solumn christening ceremony was underway.

Though everything ran smoothly after that, it was almost an hour later when Viscount Stockton and his son were able to join the ladies at one of the large dining tables, which was heavily laden with dishes of all kinds.

"The Prince Regent is in the best of spirits," Lord Stockton told the ladies, "he and Rutland being such old friends. He made sure we knew how much he would have disliked missing such a happy occasion, but how difficult their journey had been until our arrival."

Rosalind, who had observed her mama's sigh of relief when their papa appeared, now noticed how much more she seemed to enjoy herself once he was by her side. Was this what she herself would be like someday? she wondered.

"You should have been with us today, Ros," Peter said, chuckling softly. "You would have enjoyed seeing Papa quietly controlling some of the more rowdy young men and warning them not to try any pranks once we met up with the royal party. By the time he finished they were convinced that the prince would have them beheaded if they should step so much as an inch out of line. Of course, he's always had the knack of making one feel no more than three feet tall when having been caught out in some mischief or other."

He was sitting between his two sisters, and across the table he was eyeing one of the pretty daughters of a local gentleman farmer.

"You'd best take your glance away from young Bessie Birkett, if you don't want to receive the same treatment from Papa tomorrow morning," Rosalind warned him quietly. "Farmer Birkett has always been rather ambitious where his daughters are concerned, if you recall."

Peter gave her a horrified look. "Don't even think anything of that sort," he murmured in her ear. "I've not forgotten what he said when the village schoolteacher had a *tendre* for me."

The banquet hall reverberated with the sound of glasses and tankards clinking as both royal and private toasts were offered, and after more than two hours had gone by, Rosalind began to feel overheated and wished that she could escape to a cooler, quieter place. She knew she must wait, however, until the duchess rose and led some of the ladies out to see the newly decorated grand rooms, including the Regent's Gallery.

"I'm sure that you have seen the new decorations many times already," Rosalind said to her mama, "but would you mind if Judith and I join the duchess's party? I know that I have not been here since the final portion of the conversion was completed, nor has Judith."

"Of course I don't mind," Lady Stockton said happily. "Run along now, my loves, for I know you'll not want to miss anything."

As Rosalind had suspected, however, her young sister had made secret plans to join friends of her own age, so once she was assured that Judith was in the good hands of one of their mama's bosom-bows, she left the group. She did not seek to catch up with the duchess's party, however, for she now felt in need of some cooler air, and made her way toward the conservatories.

On her previous visit to the castle there had been insufficient time to view the splendid work the duke's gardeners were doing to insure that the rooms and gardens had a constant supply of plants and blooms. Now was her chance to see the many exotics procured by the duke and duchess on their travels abroad.

It was somewhat disconcerting, however, to find herself completely alone as she entered the main conservatory, but, concluding that the gardeners must be celebrating the christening in the servants' hall, she walked slowly down the aisles, then took a seat on one of the benches and inhaled the tropical fragrance of a young orange tree that was just coming into bloom.

It was extraordinarily peaceful here after the quite inordinate loudness of the festivities, and though she knew it was not at all proper for her to be out here alone, she felt completely safe. Unfortunately, there would not be many more such opportunities to visit here, for though her mama had not yet broached the subject, she was sure that very soon now she would be taken back to London for a second Season; another attempt to find her a suitable husband in the marriage mart.

In all fairness, she had to admit that she had quite enjoyed the excitement of being presented at court last year, and the time spent with her brother visiting Astley's Royal Amphitheatre, or watching a balloon ascension; and the occasions when she saw firework displays in Vauxhall Gardens, in the company of her mama and papa and some of their friends, had been quite breathtaking.

But though she knew it to be deeply disappointing to her mama, she had found herself not at all interested in any of the gentlemen who had made offers for her hand. She grimaced as she recalled how one of them, while slightly inebriated, had tried to lead her toward the dark paths at Vauxhall Gardens, and had actually attempted to put his arms around her waist. As though she would ever have permitted such a thing!

She had given him quite a scold, and then, as he had quite lost his way, she had led him back to where their party was gathered, watching the firework display. To her relief, they had not been missed, so that explanations were not necessary.

"What a delightful picture, but if I spoke of beauty among the flowers I'm sure you would think me quite lacking in originality." The voice was deep and resonant.

Rosalind gave quite a start, for she had been daydreaming and had failed to hear anyone approaching. She slowly raised her head until she had a full view of the speaker, from the tips of his spotless dress shoes to the cravat that Brummell might had admired, and a pair of large shoulders that filled out his morning coat to perfection without the slightest need of padding.

Bright blue eyes twinkled down at her from a face that was not quite handsome, for the jaw was a little too strong for that, but might better be described as craggy.

He would have been tall even without the mass of unruly, sandy-brown hair atop his head. In fact, from her seat on the bench he looked like a fortunately friendly giant.

She knew, of course, that she should not speak to any

gentleman to whom she had not been introduced, and it would have been quite simple to excuse herself and return to where the other guests congregated, for he was not showing any inclination to prevent her doing so.

"And what would you say were you being original, sir?" Her words just seemed to slip out on their own accord.

"That I must be dreaming, but if I am, then I have no wish to awake for a long time," he murmured. "May I join you?"

For answer she moved along the bench to make room for him, but knew at once that it was a mistake, for his nearness had begun to have the strangest effect upon her. There was a tightness in her chest that made her breathless, and a feeling of lethargy that prevented her from rising, as she should, and walking out of what could easily become a quite perilous situation. She wondered, faintly, if the fragrance of orange blossom might have gone to her head.

"Do you live near the castle?" he asked, making himself comfortable and stretching an arm along the back of the bench.

She nodded. "Yes, about two miles away," was all she said, for she sensed that were she to add the fact that she was the daughter of a viscount, he would have risen at once and escorted her back to the main rooms of the castle.

"The duke invited everyone for miles around to attend his son's christening," she added.

"I'm very glad he did," he said softly, letting his fingers play as lightly as butterflies on a bare piece of her shoulder.

She could not help the little shiver that passed through her at his touch.

"Are you cold?" he asked with some concern. "Would you like me to put my coat around your shoulders?"

She shook her head. "No, thank you, sir. I'm not at all cold, really," she said. As if to confirm her words, a flood of warmth suffused her whole body and when it reached her cheeks it turned them a rosy pink.

"You need not be shy, my dear," he murmured, "for I'll not harm you. You're not one of the vicar's daughters, are you?"

"No, not one of his daughters," she said, quite deliberately implying that she had some other connection with the family.

The vicar's daughters were, in fact, here today, but he must not have met any of them or he would not have asked the question, for they were all four plump and rosy-cheeked with straight blond hair, the image of their mother.

"Do you live in London, sir?" she inquired, and immediately regretted asking such an idiotic question. He must, by now, think her a veritable country bumpkin.

He nodded, kindly. "We left as soon as the fog lifted and it was quite a sight to see an escort of three hundred men come to meet us. I, for one, was glad they were friendly."

He must be part of the royal entourage, she realized, wondering just how close the connection, for she was sure she had not seen him in London though she had met the Prince Regent on a number of occasions during her come-out, last year.

She was rapidly becoming accustomed to the touch of his fingers as they stroked her neck and shoulders, and was forced to admit, if only to herself, that it was a most agreeable sensation. And, far from being cold, she could, in fact, feel a delicious warmth that seemed to steal over her entire body.

There were no sudden movements, nothing to warn her that he was taking her into his arms until she realized that was exactly where she was, and his head was a little above hers, his eyes gazing down upon her with the tenderest of expressions in them.

She felt the warmth of his breath as it touched her forehead, and he murmured, "I've wanted to do this since the moment I saw you sitting here, all alone, waiting for me, like a pale green nymph escaped from the woods."

At first his mouth felt soft, like the touch of a butterfly against her cheek, but as it trailed slowly toward her own lips it left a path of heat that quickly turned to flame as it reached its destination. At first she felt as though she could not breathe, then the problem must somehow have been solved, for she forgot everything in the surge of pleasure that swept through her. She wanted it to go on forever, but when he at last drew away, she felt cold and desolate at the loss.

"Don't tell me," he said huskily, "that you have never been kissed before? This was surely not the first time?"

She nodded, for once unable to give a coherent reply.

He seemed about to say something more when there came the sound of a door opening at the far end of the conservatory, and the gruff voices of a pair of gardeners could be heard as they slowly approached.

Rosalind was out of his arms and on her feet in a moment, and hurrying toward the door by which she had entered, her soft slippers making not a sound on the flagstone path.

Had she turned around she would have seen a look of sadness on the face of the gentleman she had just left so hurriedly, but he made no move to follow her, turning instead to talk to the gardeners and thus facilitate her escape.

At the time, she thought of little but the need to get away without being observed. But afterward, when she would recall that afternoon, a special scent always came back to her. It was the faint, subtle, masculine smell of cologne and tobacco, mingling with the exotic perfume of orange blossom and one particularly fragrant orchid.

The rest of the day passed as though in a dream, and despite her swift glance around every room she entered, she did not once catch sight of the strange gentleman with whom she had been so shamelessly forward. What she would have done had he appeared, she really did not know, for her mama, at whose side she remained for the rest of the day, would most definitely not have understood how she had come to meet him.

"You seem a little flushed, my dear," Lady Stockton said, eyeing her closely. "You don't think that you might have caught a chill on the way here, do you?"

Rosalind managed a throaty chuckle. "I know it's the middle of winter, Mama," she said, "but it was far too mild when we arrived for even Papa to catch a chill. It's quite excessively warm in here, that's all, and it will be, I suppose, as long as the Prince Regent remains."

Her father overheard her and gave an indignant snort, and he might very well have said more but at that moment the Prince

Regent approached and the ladies sank into deep curtsies.

"Delighted to meet you again, my lady," the royal prince murmured, "and your delightful daughter, of course. And who is this little charmer?"

"Allow me to present my youngest daughter, Judith, your royal highness," Lord Stockton said.

The prince, in a most benevolent mood, beamed at the young girl. "When will we see you take all London by storm, my dear?" he asked.

Before her daughter said the wrong thing, Lady Stockton put in quickly, "She's a little too young as yet, your royal highness, but in another year we'll be bringing her out."

The prince nodded. "We will look forward to seeing her, and as for you, Stockton, I must congratulate you again on the way you kept those young men in line out there today. Did my heart good to have such a grand escort to the castle."

He moved along then, and Rosalind's high color was forgotten in the exhilaration that naturally followed any meeting with royalty. Judith was quite beside herself with excitement, despite the fact that he was much older and fatter than she had expected.

It was not until Rosalind was at last alone in her bedchamber that she allowed herself to think about the all-too-brief meeting in the conservatory. She could not quite believe how rash she had been in allowing "the stranger," as she now thought of him, to take advantage of her, but try as she might, in her heart she did not regret it.

When the Season finally came around, and her mama took her to town again, though she was not quite so swift in rejecting every young man who came her way, she still could not bring herself to accept any of the gentlemen who offered for her hand.

"If you keep this up you're going to acquire a reputation for being cold, and with every justification," Lady Stockton told her as the end of her second Season approached. "What qualities are you looking for in a husband, anyway?"

Rosalind shook her head, for there was nothing to be gained by admitting to her mama that she had already met the only gentleman she had ever wanted to marry. Mama would not understand, and it had, in fact, been some time before she herself had finally conceded what it was that she had been searching for—a pair of the brightest blue, twinkling eyes, a head of sandy-brown hair, and a face that was not really handsome, but very, very special—and she was now quite sure that there was not the slightest hope of her seeing "the stranger" again.

Chapter Two

February, 1815

"I really cannot understand how you can happily remain here in Rutland, Geoffrey, and leave all the problems of the journey to London, and the opening of the town house, in my poor hands," Lady Stockton complained, still trying to convince her husband that it was nothing less than his duty to accompany her and her daughters on such a long journey.

The viscount looked up from the map of his land, which he had been contemplating before his wife came into his study and disturbed him.

"In your very capable hands, my dear," he corrected her mildly, "and with two coachmen and four outriders in attendance, not to mention our son, who is more than competent in dealing with innkeepers and the like, I cannot think how you can possibly come to harm. As I told you, I will join you for a week or so as soon as the Season begins, but there is far too much still to do on the estates for me to sit in White's every afternoon doing nothing but drink and play cards. You know quite well that neither of our girls is likely to receive an offer until the Season is well underway."

"But what am I to do if you should happen to be wrong, and some very eligible gentleman from last year desires to make an offer for Rosalind? It just might be her last chance,"

Lady Stockton avowed, "and you not there to receive it."

"If this unlikely swain has waited all winter, then I'm sure he will wait a little longer. At least until you are able to get word to me," the viscount countered, quite obviously amused at the idea. He rose and put an arm around his wife's shoulders. "Come now, my love, why don't you make sure that the girls are almost ready, for you'll need to be on your way within a half hour if you are to reach Bedford by nightfall."

Lady Stockton sniffed into a kerchief and turned watery, baleful eyes to her husband. "You know that I'm going to miss you dreadfully, don't you?" she said plaintively. "I do so dislike it when you're not there to help and advise me."

He dropped a kiss on her cheek. "I know you do, my dear," he murmured, "and I'll be with you before you've scarcely had time to turn around. I should think that Peter will ride a good part of the way. Were you aware that Rosalind actually asked me if she might ride alongside also?"

Lady Stockton smiled weakly and shook her head as he continued, "Now, I know you'll want to find out what our girls are doing all this time and I have to give final instructions to Tom Coachman. Do you think thirty minutes will do it?"

She nodded, then, well satisfied that she had at least persuaded him to come to town a little earlier than he had originally intended, she hurried out of the drawing room and up the stairs.

As usual, she went first into Rosalind's bedchamber and found her daughter standing in front of the pier mirror and gazing pensively into it. She was already dressed for the journey except for her soft green pelisse and bonnet, edged in fox fur, which had been carefully placed in readiness at the foot of the bed.

She turned to her mama with an enigmatic smile.

"I do hope that the patronesses of Almack's will realize that I'm only in London this Season to show Judith how to go along," she said softly, "for I should most heartily dislike it were they to start bringing in my direction all the young men too shy or too oafish to find a partner for themselves."

"You cannot at all blame them if they do bring gentlemen over to you if you are not dancing, my girl," Lady Stockton remarked a little dryly. "But as you have hardly missed a single dance during the last two Seasons, I cannot think that you'll have any difficulty in getting partners this year."

Unfortunately, being popular had not resulted in her daughter making a suitable match in the past, and Lady Stockton had no intention, at this late date, to in any way prevent the patronesses from introducing her to suitable gentlemen who were new in town this Season. One could never be sure just when a newcomer might not prove to be exactly the right husband for a girl like Rosalind.

The trouble was that Lady Stockton felt herself partly to blame for Rosalind refusing so many quite eligible suitors. It was she who had suggested, when Peter showed a most decided disinclination to study, that Rosalind join her brother at his studies and thus encourage him by example. Peter thrived on competition, and the plan had worked well for him, but it was unfortunate that Rosalind had grown most unbecomingly knowledgeable for a young lady. In fact, so much so, that at times she had found her to be somewhat unbiddable, and it had needed a very firm hand from Lord Stockton to control her.

Rosalind had changed a little, however, even before they went to town last year. If Lady Stockton had not known it to be impossible—for surely there had been no opportunity for her daughter to meet any gentlemen while in the country—she would have sworn that the girl was in love. By the end of the Season, however, she had to admit, once again, that Rosalind had shown no special preference for any young man, though she certainly had not lacked for suitors hoping for her hand in marriage.

"I mean to do everything I can to see that Judith enjoys herself," Rosalind said, "for that is really the only reason I agreed to another Season. She's so eager to find out what it's like, and to meet eligible gentlemen that I felt you might need help in keeping her out of trouble. It would be dreadful were she to fall in love with someone who proved to be quite unsuitable."

There was a wistful note in her daughter's voice that Lady Stockton had never noticed before, and she glanced sharply at

Rosalind, wondering once again if the girl had done just that herself, but as she had hardly let her out of her sight, it could not possibly be so. Rosalind was, in actual fact, a great deal too particular for her own good. She would never have allowed herself to fall for someone she did not know very well indeed, and hold in the highest esteem.

"What was that your papa just told me about your wishing to ride with Peter part of the way?" Lady Stockton asked, smiling despite of herself.

"Oh, I didn't really think he would agree to it, but I felt there was no harm in trying," Rosalind said, grinning. "It get's so stuffy in the carriage after a while. But I didn't at all mind when Papa said no, for Peter has promised to take me to see all kinds of things while you're busy getting Judith's gowns ordered."

Lady Stockton looked suspicious. "What kind of things does he mean to take you to see?" she asked dubiously.

"Now don't start worrying already, Mama," Rosalind admonished. "Things that you wouldn't care very much to attend, such as balloon ascensions, for there are sure to be some. And, perhaps, the Royal Circus and Astley's Amphitheatre. I've never yet seen everything I want to in St. Paul's Cathedral, and I must go to see Westminster Abbey again and to St. Margaret's Church. There are at least a half dozen places I'd like to visit this time instead of spending every single afternoon drinking tea and eating pastries."

Her mama looked askance for a moment, then appeared to reconsider, saying thoughtfully, "There's really no reason why the two of you cannot go to some of those places before the Season actually starts, but my close friends would think it very strange indeed if you were not to accompany me on afternoon calls."

Rosalind slipped her arm around Lady Stockton's thickening waist and kissed her cheek. "Of course, Mama, you know I'll not let you down," she said softly, "but this year it's Judith's turn to get attention. I just know that she'll take at once, and I'd not wish to steal any of her glory."

Almost as though she had heard her name mentioned, Judith

appeared at the door of the bedchamber, wearing a bright blue pelisse and bonnet.

"Aren't you ready yet, Rosalind?" she asked impatiently. "You know that Papa will be cross if we keep the horses waiting in this cold weather."

Rosalind and her mama exchanged amused glances. Up to this point it had always been Judith for whom they had to wait, but now she was so excited and anxious to get to London that she was ready ahead of the others.

Lady Stockton took the pelisse from the bed and helped Rosalind into it, for the girls' abigail, Hetty, along with the maids and other staff, had left before dawn so that they might reach London by nightfall, and have the bedrooms of the town house aired and ready long before the family arrived. Fortunately, an old retainer and his wife stayed at the house on Upper Brook Street through the winter months, so that the rooms never had that cold, damp feeling that pervaded so many of the London homes.

After Rosalind had taken a quick look in the mirror to be sure her bonnet was set at just the right angle, the three of them went down the stairs to kiss Lord Stockton a teary goodbye, then hurried into the waiting carriage and commenced their journey.

By the time they reached Bedford, all three ladies were feeling tired and quite chilled, for it was an icy-cold February day. The hot bricks they had started out with had cooled long before they stopped for a late luncheon, and though the innkeeper's wife had changed them for hot ones before they resumed their journey, the coach never seemed to completely warm up again.

"It's a blessing that it is dry," Lady Stockton said thankfully as they entered the inn where they were to spend the night, "for if it had snowed all day we would have been in a fine mess."

"I don't know," Rosalind said cheerfully, "as I recall this is an excellent inn with large, comfortable rooms and spotlessly clean beds. Not at all a bad place to be snowbound. Didn't we have a suite last time we were here, Mama?"

Ignoring such a dreadful possibility, Lady Stockton said, "Yes, we did, and we're supposed to have the very same one booked again for the three of us, with Peter close by. I'll order a good hot supper to be served upstairs, and then we'll all have an early night."

Judith looked disappointed. "Why can't we have a private dining room downstairs?" she asked plaintively. "I've never stayed in an inn before, and I did so want to see what a taproom looked like."

"We couldn't enter a taproom, you silly goose," her sister teased. "It's a place with a bar, where only men and very low-class women are allowed."

"And how would you know that, Rosalind?" Lady Stockton asked sharply. "It seems to me that Peter has been teaching you a little too much for your own good."

Just then the landlady came bustling up, recognized Lady Stockton at once, and led the party up the stairs and into their suite of rooms.

When hot water to wash in and a satisfactory dinner had been ordered, Lady Stockton made certain that fires were burning brightly in the bedroom fireplaces besides the one in the private parlor that separated them. Then, when she was sure that everything they needed for their stay was at hand, to Rosalind's dismay she returned to the previous topic of conversation.

"As I was saying," she went on, "Peter has taught you things that no gentleman would expect his wife to be aware of, and it might be best if you put some of the more unladylike ones completely from your mind."

"Oh, it wasn't Peter who told me," Rosalind said airily. "The last time we were here I rose early and took a peek inside the taproom. There was no one there except the barman who was washing and polishing an enormous number of glasses and, to his credit, he did tell me also that it was not the kind of place for a nice young lady to be."

"I should think so," Lady Stockton said sharply, but she could not help but smile at her daughter's curiosity. "You know, I'm sure, that in my day it would never have occurred to ladies of your age to leave their mother's side for a moment when staying in a place of this sort."

"I know, Mama, but you must agree that when you were young the gowns that we all now wear would have been considered quite indecent, particularly when dampened petticoats are worn beneath them," Rosalind asserted. "Times do change you know, Mama."

"But not always for the better," Lady Stockton stoutly declared. "If a daughter of mine should ever try to go out with dampened petticoats, I would send her back to the country that very night."

"Don't tease yourself with such a thought," Rosalind said with a soft chuckle, placing an arm around her mama's slender shoulders and giving her a hug. "I can think of nothing more uncomfortable than a damp gown, and I am sure that Judith feels the same."

There was a light tap on the door and Peter came in, still dressed in his riding habit and heavy cloak.

"Everything's secure for the night, and I've given instructions to the coachman that we must be ready to depart in the morning by ten o'clock at the latest," he told them. "How do you feel, Mama? Not too tired by the journey, I hope."

"I had grown quite chilly in the carriage," Lady Stockton admitted, "but now that I've thawed out a little I feel very much better, and I do believe that this really is the same suite of rooms that we stayed in last year when your papa was with us. Hot water will be here at any moment, I should think, and I also ordered a bottle of sherry to be sent up, for I feel we could all do with a little inner warmth."

"Then I'd best be off and get out of these things, for you'll not want me dining with you in my dirt," Peter said. "I'm just two doors away, so I won't be long once the hot water arrives. You needn't order port for me, though, for when I came in I ran into a couple of fellows I knew at Oxford, and I arranged to have a drink with them after dinner tonight.''

Rosalind frowned, for she knew only too well how Peter's one drink could lead to another, and then another, but Lady Stockton just smiled benignly and said, ''How very nice for you to have some male companionship, dear. I'm so glad your papa selected this inn for us to stop at, for it does seem to have an excellent clientele.''

The fire ablaze in the hearth, the inner warmth of the glass of sherry, and then a most satisfying dinner of mock turtle soup, poached fish with sauce piquante, roast green goose, and broiled lamp chops, had the effect of making the ladies quite pleasantly sleepy.

Within a half hour of Peter wishing them a good night and leaving to meet his friends, all three of them retired to their bedchambers, Lady Stockton falling into a sound sleep almost before her head touched the feather pillow. The two girls were sharing a bedchamber, and at first Judith seemed inclined to talk, but soon her eyes began to close and then she also fell into a deep sleep.

Rosalind, however, although quite tired, was kept awake by an uneasy feeling about Peter, and it had been for this reason that she had insisted on taking the bed nearest to the door.

She kept dozing and wakening for a while, then, just as she felt herself nodding off again, she heard the sound of the parlor door opening and the whisper of male voices.

Reaching for her dressing gown, she quickly slipped it on, then quietly opened the door to the parlor where an oil lamp had been left burning.

Three men were standing in the parlor doorway, and she recognized the middle one as her brother, Peter, but it seemed that he was having difficulty staying on his feet. They came further into the parlor then looked up and saw her standing watching them.

''Oh, I didn't realize his little wife was waiting up for him,'' one of the men whispered to his companion, ''did you? We'd best leave him in her hands.''

"You'd best do no such thing," Rosalind said as loudly as she dared without wakening her mama. "This isn't his chamber and I'm not his wife but his sister. His chamber is two doors away, and he must have the key on him somewhere."

It was soon obvious that neither of the two men was faring much better than her brother, so she went to the open parlor door and said sharply, "Come along now, bring him out here and I'll look in his pocket for the key. You don't want to wake our mama, do you?"

"No, ma'am, we don't want to do that," one of them whispered, then painfully slowly they walked him out of the parlor and started along the corridor. When they reached the second door, Rosalind felt in Peter's coat pockets until she had the key in her hand, and once she had unlocked and pushed open the door, she found, much to her relief, that the oil lamps were burning brightly in a bedchamber she recognized as her brother's by the bags that bore his initials.

"Help me get his coat off," she whispered, then realized that there was no longer a need to do so, and added in a normal voice, "and I would appreciate it if you would remove his trousers and get him into bed while my back is turned."

"You're really his sister, ma'am?" the dark-haired young man asked, articulating carefully.

"Yes, I am," she said, turning to face the door, "and I'd like to get back to my own bed, so if you would just do as I ask, I'll make sure that all the candles are out and the fire banked up properly before I leave. I'll take the key with me and come back in the morning to wake him, for we're planning an early start."

She heard the sound of a great deal of effort being made, for by now Peter was asleep in their arms, and a few minutes later one of the men touched her shoulder.

"He'll sleep it off now, ma'am," he said, his voice sounding much more sober than it had before, "and I do beg your pardon for frightening you when we came in like that."

"That's quite all right," Rosalind said, "and if I should meet you again in London, I do hope you will not admit to having seen me before.''

''Yes, ma'am,'' he said, a faint twinkle in his eyes, ''only wish I had a sister with half your spunk. We'll wait outside and see you safely back to your chamber.''

Rosalind found a piece of paper and wrote a note so that Peter would not be concerned should he wake up before she got there in the morning, then she made sure the fire was safe, doused the candles, and locked the door, slipping the key into the pocket of her dressing gown.

The two young men had waited, and, a little shakily, they escorted her back to the suite and stayed outside until she closed the door and locked it. Rosalind paused a moment to be sure her mama was not going to suddenly appear, then she crept back into her own bedchamber.

The sound of steady breathing persuaded her that her sister had not woken, and within a few minutes she, also, fell into a sound sleep, waking a little after seven o'clock, and once more creeping along the corridor to her brother's room.

She was just about to unlock the door when the gentleman who had been the more sober of the two last night appeared, fully dressed for the road and holding a glass of something in his hand.

''Why don't you hurry back to your own chamber before anyone sees you,'' he suggested, holding out his hand for the key. ''I have something here that will make him feel much better in a little while.''

With a grateful smile, Rosalind gave him the key, and was back in their suite almost before he had opened the door. As it happened, she was just in time, for as she bent over the fire to give it a poke and get a blaze going again, the door to her mama's bedchamber opened and Lady Stockton came out, yawning sleepily.

''I was just coming out to do the same thing, my dear,'' she said. ''Put some more wood on, would you, and we'll at least be nice and warm before we leave. Did you notice if it was a fine day?''

"No, for I slept in the bed nearest the door," Rosalind told her, "but I have a feeling that it's going to be an excellent day."

"I'll ring for hot water," Lady Stockton said, "but we needn't waken Judith until it comes. I do hope that Peter did not stay up too late last evening, but he's a sensible young man and I'm sure he did not. I know that he feels most responsible for us in his father's absence."

It was not until they reached the town house on Upper Brook Street, much later in the day, that Peter had a chance to speak to Rosalind with a modicum of privacy.

Lady Stockton and Judith had gone upstairs to change for dinner, and Rosalind was about to do so when Peter placed a hand on her arm.

"I apprehend that I've much to be grateful to you for, Ros," he said quietly. "I had just read the note you left in case I woke before you came along, and when the door started to open I thought it was you, but I'm glad it wasn't, for I was feeling pretty awful."

"I thought you might be, but the gentleman to whom I gave the key said he had something that would help you," she murmured sympathetically. "Was it of any assistance?"

"I didn't deserve it, but I don't know how I'd have managed to stay on my horse today without it," he told her, looking unhappy, and Rosalind felt sorry for him, for she knew how much he would have hated to have let his father down.

"I just got back to the suite before Mama came out of her bedchamber, and I don't believe Judith woke all night," she said, "so no one other than me and two unknown gentlemen know anything about it. You do know that it will stay that way, don't you?"

Her brother nodded. "I had to say thanks, though, for I'd gone off with one of the keys to the suite, by mistake, and I'd never have lived it down had Mama got up instead of you and seen me in that state. You made a big impression on both of those gentlemen, and one in particular, but he promises not to recognize you when you next meet.''

"Oh, no, you can't mean that I really am likely to meet a man who saw me first in a nightcap and dressing gown?'' Rosalind asked in dismay. "I felt sure they were going north and not proceeding to London.''

"They were going north this morning, but they will be back in London for the start of the Season, and you're sure to meet.'' He grinned a little painfully. "I'll not tell you who they are, and we'll see if you recognize them, for I understand they were in little better shape than I was.''

"You forget that I saw one of them this morning, and he looked very different from what he did last night, but I did not,'' Rosalind said. "I would be dreadfully embarrassed were I to meet them again at a ball or something. Will they be at Almack's, do you think?''

"Most certainly,'' Peter assured her cheerfully. "And wouldn't it be funny if one of the patronesses brought them over to meet you?''

"Not for me, it wouldn't,'' she said, "but perhaps the other one will look so different I'll never know him.''

"It's not the other one who was so impressed with you, Ros. It's the one you met again this morning, and I believe that you were one of the reasons why he came along to help me the next morning, as he did.'' Peter was quite obviously amused at her discomfiture.

She sighed. "I suppose that's what comes of being kind to intoxicated gentlemen, but I would have thought that, with the way I ordered them about, they'd think of me more as a harridan than anything else,'' she said, then glanced at the clock on the mantelpiece. "Oh dear, I'd forgotten that I get to use Hetty first. I'd best hurry upstairs right away or Judith is going to be quite justifiably angry with me.''

As she quickly left the room, she thought briefly about Peter's friend. He was, no doubt, a pleasant enough gentleman when sober, but she had no particular wish to meet him again in

London. In fact, the only man she had any wish to meet there was the one she had come to think of as "the stranger," and by now he was probably married and no longer living in London but on a country estate somewhere.

Chapter Three

The morning following their arrival, Rosalind awoke early after a refreshing night's sleep and quickly donned her old riding habit which, with town so obviously empty of society, was quite good enough for now.

She hurried down the stairs, hoping that Peter had not forgotten his promise to take her for a ride in the park, and wondering, supposing he had, if she dare go out by herself with only a groom in attendance. There was no doubt that Mama would become most upset were she to do so and be caught out, and she quickly decided against it, for it would be a poor way to start their stay in town.

Fortunately, there was little need to put this to the test, for Peter was down before her and sipping a first cup of coffee in the breakfast room.

"I've already ordered the horses brought around, Ros," he told her with a grin, "so you'd best look sharp about it if you want a cup of coffee before we leave. It's much too cold at this hour to leave them standing."

She ran her fingers through the hair he had just spent the better part of fifteen minutes trying to arrange in a windswept style—something she would never have dared do had he not been going to put on a hat. Then she moved swiftly away as he jumped to his feet, smoothing his rumpled curls and scowling at her.

"You'll do that once too often, young Ros, when I'm not feeling quite so amiable," he warned, wagging a finger in her direction, "and you'll go across my knee for it."

Rosalind knew full well that she had nothing to fear, for her brother had never laid a hand on her despite some of the quite dreadful tricks she had played upon him as a little girl, though he frequently made threats. And he had never once told of her misdeeds and got her into trouble with their parents. They were the best of friends, and she would miss him most dreadfully when he finally found himself a wife and set up in a home of his own.

The coffee was hot and bitter, and she had time to swallow no more than half a cup before putting on her riding gloves and following Peter out of the room.

He had been quite right, for it was extremely cold, and she shivered a little as she hurried down the steps just as the groom appeared with the horses, her breath clearly visible on the early morning air.

Once mounted, she leaned over to murmur soothingly in her mare's ear before following Peter along Upper Brook Street and into Park Lane. The traffic was light at this hour, and soon they were in the park and able to warm up with a lengthy gallop.

"It's really much too early to expect anyone I know to be in town," Rosalind remarked, as they continued at a slower pace. "Mama always believes that arriving here so soon gives her first choice of materials and such, before the ladies of higher rank descend upon the modistes with their demands."

"Just because you're not so conscious of rank as she is, doesn't mean that Mama is wrong, you know," Peter warned. "This way she gets exactly what she wants and does not put anyone else's nose out of joint. You could benefit by learning a little tactful behavior from her, you know, Ros."

She grinned sheepishly. "I suppose I could, and I really should try to acquire a great deal more fortitude. But you haven't been through all this twice already, Peter, as I have. They call it the Marriage Mart, and that is exactly what it is, putting young ladies up for sale to the highest bidder."

"Do you know of a better way to find a suitable spouse?" her brother asked quite sharply. "You should be grateful that Mama and Papa have not run out of patience with you already. If they were not so happy themselves, they would have forced you into accepting someone long before now. Surely you cannot wish to become an old maid, playing with your nephews and nieces instead of your own children?"

Rosalind turned an earnest face toward him. "Don't you start bullying me, too, Peter," she begged. "It isn't that I haven't considered carefully each and every gentleman who has proposed marriage to me. It's just that I know exactly what I want most in a husband, and I haven't found it in any one of them yet."

Her brother reached for her hand and squeezed it. "I'm not bullying you now, and I never have. Just don't wait too long, that's all, or you'll find yourself high on the shelf. Do you have to go shopping with Mama and Judith this afternoon?"

"Not if you have a better suggestion," Rosalind said hopefully, thankful that he had dropped the topic of marriage for now. "Their first visit will be to the modiste, and I can easily prevail upon Mama to take care of Judith first, I know."

"Then let's go to Westminster Abbey and St. Margaret's Church," he suggested, noticing how the light had come back into her eyes again as he had meant it to. "It should be comparatively quiet there as yet. Mama will be using the carriage, but we can get a hackney on the corner."

They set out for another gallop, but had gone only a short distance when they heard a shout, and a well-dressed gentleman, mounted on a magnificent white stallion, went flying past them, grinning widely. He slowed to a trot, and as they almost caught up with him he turned to show off his mount.

"Well met, George," Peter said to his friend, Lord Cleary. "And what a beauty you've got there. I did not expect you to be in town for some time. You remember m'sister, Rosalind, of course."

"How could I forget?" the young man said gallantly, still grinning and raising his hat. "At your service, ma'am."

Rosalind smiled at her brother's friend, Lord Cleary, then gazed admiringly at his mount as he turned back to Peter.

"Just got him last week at Tattersall's," Lord Cleary said. "For once it paid to come to town early, but it wasn't just chance. I'd heard that old Grimsby was up to his eyes in debt and selling his entire stable, so I came up on the chance of finding a bargain. If he'd been able to wait until the Season was in full swing he could have almost doubled what he got for everything."

It was more than obvious that Lord Cleary was an excellent horseman for though the stallion was quite fresh he had him under excellent control.

"You've no idea how glad I am to see you in town so early, Peter," he said, "for I was beginning to think I'd have a very lean time for the next week or two. Do you have plans for this afternoon?"

Peter smiled a little ruefully. "I do, but I'm afraid you might not wish to fall in with them," he told his friend. "I've just arranged to take Rosalind to see Westminster Abbey and St. Margaret's Church."

Lord Cleary looked puzzled for a moment, then his ready grin returned. "What a splendid idea," he declared. "Mind if I join you? I've not been there in years, and though I prefer St. Paul's, I'd not at all mind taking another look at the Abbey."

"At least you'll not now need to stay home this evening," Rosalind said to her brother, then turned back to Lord Cleary. "Has your family come up to London at this time also?"

"No, they'll not be here for a couple of weeks or more yet," he said, "so I'm staying in rooms nearby, rather than open up the house, but I am using our own stables, for I came up to town in my phaeton."

"If you're willing to take potluck, I know that you'll be welcome to have dinner with us, George," Peter put in. "It won't be grand, of course, for Mama hasn't had time to get things in order as yet, but I know she'll be glad to see you again."

"I couldn't take advantage of her kindness when you've only

just got here—'' Lord Cleary started to protest, when Rosalind interrupted.

"You've always been a favorite of Mama's, and she'd be most upset if we did not invite you,'' she told him. "Just you see, she'll ask you herself when she finds that you're in town alone.''

"Very well,'' he said. "And now I'll give Rogue here another run, and don't you suggest a race, Peter, for we can't leave Rosalind alone without so much as a groom.''

It was more than obvious that Peter was disappointed, but there would be other mornings like this, and he was not one to grumble.

"I'll call for you at, say, two o'clock?'' Lord Cleary suggested, and when Peter nodded he let the impatient stallion have its head, disappearing from sight in what seemed like no time at all.

"I feel terribly guilty,'' Rosalind said when they turned back toward Park Lane. "I'm sure you would have preferred to go somewhere far more exciting, but I must say that George did not seem to at all mind going to the Abbey.''

"He wouldn't,'' Peter averred. "He's the best of good fellows, and he's always had a preference for your company. You see, his own sisters tended to be girlish and giggly, and you behave like one of us when we're all together.'' His eyes twinkled. "Not quite like one of us, of course, but you're comfortable to be with.''

The breakfast room showed no signs of use when they entered, after having washed some of the dirt from their hands, but Lady Stockton joined them in just a few minutes and was delighted that Lord Cleary was to dine with them.

"I do believe he is quite the nicest of your friends, and until his mama comes to town you may bring him here to dine any time you wish,'' she told her son, then turned to Rosalind. "But I do not recall excusing you from joining your sister and me today. You will need some new gowns, you know.''

"Now, Mama, you know that you'd much rather concentrate all your attention on Judith at first, for she's going to need so very many gowns as soon as the Season begins, not to mention her presentation gown, of course. I'll gladly join you as soon as most of Judith's needs are taken care of,'' Rosalind assured her, rising and going over to the sideboard where an array of covered dishes awaited their pleasure. "Now, tell me what I can help get for you.''

Lady Stockton smiled, knowing quite well that, as usual, Rosalind would have her way. But she was, without doubt, the most helpful and considerate of her three daughters, besides being the prettiest. And George Cleary was not at all a bad match if it should happen that he had taken a fancy to her, which might very well be the case, for when was the last time that he had been in Westminster Abbey? she wondered. She was sure it must have been when a tutor had taken him there for an outing.

Had she been able to observe the three of them later that afternoon as they wandered through the Abbey, she might have been even more hopeful, for though they would never have shown frivolity inside a house of God, once they were outdoors again they laughed hilariously as one and then another of them imitated the various poses in which the statues had been carved.

"It would seem that not one more statue or monument could be squeezed in,'' Rosalind remarked as they stood looking once more at the Abbey in all its splendor. "The Prince Regent and his brothers must surely be carved in miniature when their turns come around. It's a pity, though, that so much is crowded inside, for from the outside it looks so magnificent, but the glorious lines of the building are sadly obscured from within.''

Agreeing completely, Lord Cleary added, "They'll probably start throwing out some of the older, lesser known ones soon, to make more room.''

St. Margaret's Church appeared very small after their tour of Westminster Abbey, but it had been the church of the Commons ever since the year 1614, and members of the House were still *ex officio* parishioners. Though it now showed signs of needing considerable restoration, it had a cozy familiarity and, following Rosalind's lead, the two gentlemen knelt in prayer for a moment before leaving.

"I say, Peter, how about taking your sister to Gunter's in

Berkeley Square for ices? It would surely make an appropriate finish to a delightful afternoon," Lord Cleary suggested, as they stepped into his carriage.

Rosalind could not conceal a slight shiver at the thought, for though the sun was out it gave little warmth at this time of year.

Noticing this, Peter grinned and replied, "By all means, but I think we'd best step down and into the tea shop or Rosalind might easily freeze to death."

"Oh, by all means," Lord Cleary said. "I'd not given a thought to having ices outside at this time of year. Tea and pastries, of course, will be much more the thing on a day like this."

As they sipped the fragrant tea and nibbled on Italian pastries, Rosalind could not help but wish all teas could be so light and gay, instead of the dreary ones she would soon be attending with Judith and their mama. At the ladies' teas there was always bound to be gossip and sly remarks made by some about her having yet another Season, instead of the affectionate teasing of her present companions.

Although she deliberately prolonged the treat, it could not last forever, and soon they stepped into the carriage once more for the short ride back to Upper Brook Street, and their farewells were brief for they would be dining together again in just a few hours.

It went without question that Lord Cleary found dinner that evening to be most entertaining. For one thing, it was the first time he had seen Judith in years—and the younger girl's first encounter with a real Regency buck.

When she heard they were to have a gentleman guest at supper, Judith made first claim to Hetty, who was to be shared by the two sisters, and had her spend almost all the time available before the dinner bell sounded in putting up her hair, taking it down, and then putting it up again.

After waiting for the abigail to appear, and then dressing herself except for the fastening of her gown, Rosalind finally stormed into her sister's bedchamber to find out just what was going on.

Seeing her, Judith took a firm hold upon Hetty's hand and refused to allow her to even go over and fasten up her sister's gown, leaving Rosalind no alternative but to go along the corridor to their mama's bedchamber.

Lady Stockton gasped when she saw the state of undress in which her daughter had traversed the hallway between the chambers.

"What is the meaning of this, Rosalind?" she asked, visibly shocked. "Surely you have more sense of decency than to wander around in that condition, particularly when we have a guest here already for supper."

"I am just attempting to illustrate the effect that one abigail between two sisters will have on this occasion, and no doubt all future occasions when we are not spending a simple evening at home alone," Rosalind said, not even trying to hide her angry indignation.

At a sign from her mistress, Lady Stockton's own abigail, Manners, hastened over to Rosalind and was rapidly fastening her gown while the latter expressed her annoyance in no uncertain terms.

She went on, "I just went into my sister's bedchamber to see what was going on, and Judith forcibly held the girl so that she could not aid me in any way."

"But Hetty is supposed to come to you first," Lady Stockton protested. "Did Peter perhaps delay you downstairs?"

"No, Mama, he did not," Rosalind said. "In fact, I came up before Judith did, but I suppose she had made arrangements with Hetty in advance. And don't blame the abigail, for she has probably been in a stew about deserting me this past half hour. Unless you wish to delay dinner, I suggest you ask for a tray to be sent to my bedchamber, for I cannot appear downstairs with my hair in this state of disarray."

"I've finished with Manners now, and she'll make a quicker job of getting you ready than Hetty could. I'll delay dinner for fifteen minutes and will deal with Judith myself later, so don't start quarreling in front of our guest, even if your sister starts it," Lady Stockton warned, knowing that the latter was a distinct possibility.

"Come along, Miss Rosalind," the usually austere Manners said, putting an arm around the slender waist and steering her toward the door. "I've been just aching to get my hands into that lovely hair of yours."

Fifteen minutes later, looking most elegant with curls piled high on her head and a few seductive strands curling about her ears, Rosalind descended the stairs and entered the drawing room.

Lady Stockton gave her an approving glance that told her she was most certainly in looks this evening.

George Cleary picked up a glass of sherry from the tray on the sideboard and brought it over to her, then raised his own glass.

"To a very lovely lady," he murmured, admiration evident in his eyes, "and may this Season bring you everything you desire."

A pink flush tinged Rosalind's cheeks, for in the past she had always regarded him as simply a good friend of her brother, rather than one of her own admirers.

"I'd be happier if only I knew what it is that I desire," she told him softly, wishing for just a moment that she might fall in love with this nice young man.

From across the room, Judith was scowling at her sister for monopolizing their guest.

"That's not at all the way to attract a young man," her brother murmured in his younger sister's ear. "Not that I think you could ever stand a chance, for George has always had a *tendre* for Rosalind though she never seemed to notice."

"She appears to be noticing now," snapped Judith. "You can tell by the way she's gazing into his eyes."

"And I can see the green-eyed monster in yours," he returned sharply. "You'd best be careful, for an obvious jealousy of Rosalind does not at all become you."

He moved away as a stern-faced Lady Stockton came over.

"I shall have a good deal to say to you, young lady, when our guest leaves," she said quietly. "I'm surprised to find that a daughter of mine would behave in such a way. If this child-ishness persists I shall be forced to conclude that you are not yet mature enough for a come-out, and will send you back home until you learn to behave in a more seemly manner."

"I didn't do anything." Judith pouted. "It was just that Hetty was all thumbs and could not seem to arrange my hair becom-ingly. I did not realize how late it was getting."

"Well, it will not happen again, for I have told the girl that she is to always attend to Rosalind's needs first, unless I give her instructions to the contrary," Lady Stockton said. "And we'll have no further discussion of the matter at this time, for you are causing me to neglect our guest. Come, we will join the others now."

The pout had gone from Judith's face by the time they had crossed the room, and a carefully practiced half smile had taken its place.

"How grown-up you look, Judith," George Cleary said kindly. "I do believe that I might not have known you had I seen you outside of this house."

"I wanted to make my come-out last year," she said rather breathlessly, "but Mama would not hear of it, though I know that some young ladies do come out at seventeen."

"I know, for my own sisters were equally impatient," he said with an understanding smile. "And much too soon, it seemed, they were married with all the responsibilities of a household upon their shoulders. Make the most of this time, my dear, for life will never again be quite so wonderful and carefree."

Judith murmured something in response and he politely bent his head to listen more intently.

"Did you have a successful expedition today?" Rosalind asked her mama. "Were you able to find the fabrics and designs so early in the year?"

"Oh, yes," Lady Stockton assured her, "for I sent a note to the modiste before we left for London. She had everything waiting for us, which is why I have used only her services for so many years. And did you enjoy your afternoon?'' she asked, her eyes twinkling. "I would gravely doubt that Westminster Abbey has changed one jot since last you were there.''

"Of course it hasn't,'' Rosalind said, smiling in turn. "But I always find something there that I missed before, or have forgotten about. You should not have allowed Peter's tutor to teach me if you had not wished me to enjoy such places.''

"Unfortunately, we cannot correct such mistakes, once made,'' her mama murmured softly, "but I'm not sure even now that I would wish you to be other than you are. Would you like me to hire another girl to look after you? I'd not like to see a repetition of this evening's problem occur on a night when we were attending an important ball.''

Rosalind smiled and shook her head. "I really don't think it's necessary, Mama. If Hetty sets out my clothes ahead of time, all I need is to have my hair arranged and my gown fastened. And I'll get an early start so that I shall have a spare moment or two to look in on Judith and see that all is well before I go down each night. I was just cross as crabs tonight because I could not even get my gown fastened.''

Lady Stockton gave her daughter a warm smile, for that was indeed a mild way to describe how irate she had felt at the time. "Very well,'' she said. "But if it begins to be a problem you will let me know, won't you?''

As Rosalind nodded in agreement, Walters, the butler, announced that dinner was served, and Lord Cleary offered his arm to Lady Stockton while Peter followed with a sister on each of his arms.

"When do you expect your mama to come up to London?'' Lady Stockton asked Lord Cleary. "I'm so looking forward to seeing her again, for though your sisters are all now off of her hands, I know how much she still enjoys the excitement of a London Season.''

"She should be here within the month,'' he told her. "Winters in the north are inevitably cold and somewhat dreary for her, and it always seems that London suits her much better, despite the damp.''

Lady Stockton looked pleased with the news, for Lady Cleary was an old friend who had married a gentleman of considerable wealth, most of which had been inherited by this personable young man on his father's death a couple of years ago. It was more than likely that he had now decided to look for a wife, or had been bullied into doing so by his three married sisters. From the way he had looked at Rosalind, she felt sure they would be seeing a great deal of him this Season.

With only five at table, conversation was general and quite gay, and afterward, though Lady Stockton would have dearly enjoyed a game of cards, she took out her sewing basket and stitched away at a piece of needlepoint while the young people played a noisy game of whist in which Judith's voice could clearly be heard above the others.

When the tea tray was brought in, she noticed Judith's flushed face and reminded herself that the child needed some direction as to ladylike behavior at a card table—and that a proper young lady never, even in jest, told a guest he was a scoundrel and an unscrupulous cheat. She could not help but wonder, once more, if she had made a mistake in trying to have two daughters in the Marriage Mart at the same time.

Chapter Four

"Miss Rosalind has breakfasted and gone out again? What do you mean, Walters? You must be mistaken." Lady Stockton was extremely agitated, for she had hurried down to breakfast in order to remind her older daughter that she must go this morning for a final fitting of her gown. She surely could not have forgotten, with Almack's opening ball just two days away!

"She went off with Mr. Peter, my lady," Walters assured her. "Must be half an hour ago, and she did say she'd be back before eleven."

She moved toward the door again, as though meaning to return to her bedchamber, then turned back and looked at the most appetizing dishes of food set out on the sideboard. A bowl of creamy porridge was being kept warm in a pan of hot water, a platter of crispy bacon looked most appetizing as did a plate of poached eggs, garnished with watercress and surrounded by slices of sweet home-fed ham, and there was a rack of freshly baked bread toasted to perfection.

Walters held out her chair, "Won't you allow me to seat you, my lady, and get you a bit of breakfast?"

His face had lost some of its usual austere expression for he had always had a soft spot for his mistress. "I've always found that things have a way of seeming better when you've had something to eat, ma'am."

She sighed. "You're quite right, Walters, they do. You may get me a poached egg, a slice of ham, and some toast to begin with, and a cup of tea, of course."

He brought the tea first, as always, then prepared the plate she had asked for.

"I'm sure Miss Rosalind will be back when she said, my lady, for she always is," he reminded her.

Lady Stockton smiled. "Of course she is, Walters," she said. "I've rarely known her not to be back at the time she said she would. And she'll probably be quite prepared to turn around and go right out again with me to the modiste. At her age she does not seem to tire the way we older ones do."

"That's right, my lady," Walters said. "Is there anything else I can get for you?"

"Just find the newspaper for me, if you can, unless my children took it with them. Ah, I see you've got it," she murmured as he produced it from behind one of the chairs. "Things are never where they should be when you have a family home."

After he had left, she read the newspaper while she ate, not at all minding a solitary breakfast for it was likely to be the most peaceful part of the day. If Rosalind would not be back until eleven, she would have time to go through to the kitchen and make sure that everything had been procured for the small dinner she had planned for tomorrow evening, before going to Almack's. Her sister and brother-in-law, Lord and Lady Thomas and their son Bernard would be there, of course, as well as Lady Cleary with George, and one of Peter's friends to even up the party.

She looked up from the paper as she heard her youngest daughter hurrying down the stairs, then waited patiently until she came bursting into the breakfast room.

"Oh, Mama, you must come at once," Judith said, in great agitation. "That stupid Hetty has just ruined the gown I am to wear tomorrow night!"

Although Lady Stockton realized that this was, in all probability, the grossest of exaggerations, she rose at once, put an arm around her daughter, and walked with her into the hall and up the stairs.

On entering the bedchamber, she realized at once what had happened, for the gown was on the bed and there was a distinct scorch mark on the bottom frill. Hetty had her back to the door, but when the abigail turned around, and Lady Stockton saw the tears and the bright red mark across one cheek, she found it difficult to contain her anger with her daughter.

"I wish to speak to Hetty alone," she said to Judith. "Go into my sitting room and stay there until I join you."

Not until the door had closed behind her daughter did she say another word, then she examined the gown closely to make sure the scorch mark was the only damage. After that, she turned to the abigail and asked her, "How long have you worked for me, Hetty?"

"More than three years, milady, since Miss Patricia had her come-out," the girl said, almost in a whisper.

"And this is the first time you have ever damaged any of my daughters' gowns, isn't it?" Lady Stockton asked quietly.

"Oh, yes, milady, I never did anything like this before," the girl said, overcome with misery.

"Then I cannot think it so terrible a crime to warrant tears," Lady Stockton said kindly. "I will be visiting the modiste this morning with Miss Rosalind, and if you can pack the gown back into its box, I will take it with me. I will ask for a new panel to be inserted in the frill and no one will ever notice. We will have it back by tomorrow morning, I am sure, if not earlier. Now dry your tears and get the gown ready for me to take."

"Oh, milady, thank you ever so much," Hetty said, dropping her a curtsy, and she was about to say more but was interrupted by Lady Stockton.

"Just one thing. If my daughter, or anyone else in this house ever slaps you again, no matter what the reason, you are to come to me at once. Is that clear?" There was anger in Lady Stockton's voice, but it was not directed at the girl.

"She didn't . . . " the girl began, then apparently realized the futility of a lie and said, "Yes, milady."

Lady Stockton swept out of the bedchamber and into her sitting room, where Judith sat calmly playing with a letter opener.

"I thought I had cured you of slapping people when you were a little girl, Judith, but it appears that you have continued the distasteful habit," Lady Stockton began, after she had closed the door firmly behind her.

"I didn't do anything, and she's lying if she says I did," Judith said, jumping to her feet.

"Don't accuse Hetty of your own offense, Judith. I could see your finger marks on her cheek. And if tomorrow night were anything but the opening ball at Almack's, and your absence would cause comment, I would forbid you to attend because of such conduct," Lady Stockton said sternly. "If you should ever show such deplorable behavior again, I will send you back to the country for the balance of the Season. This morning, I am going to the modiste with Rosalind, and I will take your gown with me and have a small panel inserted in place of the scorched piece. And now the matter is closed."

Judith, who had burst into tears at the threat of being banished from London, stammered an apology and ran from the room, to Lady Stockton's obvious relief. Once she was alone, she sank into an armchair and closed her eyes to ward off the megrim that threatened.

She was sleeping when Rosalind came looking for her just before eleven. Having heard the whole story from a now reptentant Judith, she was reluctant to waken her mama, but knew that Lady Stockton would be more than a little cross if she did not.

As she said a soft, "Mama," Lady Stockton opened her eyes and looked about her.

"I believe I fell asleep for a few minutes, my dear," she remarked. "Are you ready to go to have your gown fitted?"

"Yes, the carriage will be outside in just a few minutes," Rosalind told her, adding, "Judith's gown is in the hall ready to be taken with us."

"You are such a comfort, my dear. I don't know what I would

do without you. Where did you go this morning?'' Lady Stockton asked. "I assume it was somewhere with Peter.''

Rosalind nodded. "After we ate breakfast, he told me that there was to be a balloon ascension. He took me there in a hackney and we were just in time to see it go up.''

She dare not tell her mama how very much she had wanted to get into the basket and go sailing with them over the tops of the trees, for Lady Stockton would have forbidden it at once. If she should ever have the chance to go up in one, she would take it in a minute, but could not possibly do so if her mama had specifically said she must not.

"When your papa comes to town, I mean to ask him to buy Peter a curricle or some such vehicle, for I do not at all like him taking you about in hackneys,'' Lady Stockton told her. "You'd best not let Peter know of my intention, however, in case Lord Stockton should refuse.''

They left then, and the modiste found no difficulty at all in having both Judith's and Rosalind's gowns ready before they had completed their other shopping. They were back in ample time for tea, and though she was not formally receiving that day, Lady Stockton was delighted when George Cleary called and brought his mama, who had just last night arrived in town.

While the two old friends eagerly sought to catch up on all the gossip since they last met, George did not fail to ensure that, at Almack's tomorrow evening, he could have a waltz and the dance before supper with Rosalind, and a cotillion with Judith.

Judith's eyes sparkled as she told her mama, after the guests had departed, that she already had five dances reserved, and Rosalind tried hard to hide her amusement as her sister said in awed tones that they were with "four lords and a knight, not a plain gentleman among them.''

"You'll soon find out,'' Rosalind told her, "that all the lords are not necessarily gentlemen, and that many of the plain gentlemen are far wealthier and more highly respected than some of the lords, or they would not be permitted in Almack's.''

"But I simply couldn't be just a plain Mrs. Someone,'' Judith said in horror. "After all, Papa is a viscount and I don't think he would allow it."

"That would all depend upon who the man was," Lady Stockton said dryly, though her eyes twinkled. "We would naturally prefer you to marry someone of rank, provided he would make a good husband, but why don't we wait and see if anyone asks for you, before making that decision?"

"Oh, I'm not going to be like Ros," Judith said airily. "She's much too particular by far, but it's all right by me if she never marries, for she'll probably make a wonderful maiden aunt to mine and Patricia's children. She'll be able to come and stay with them while my husband and I go off on a tour of Europe."

"Judith, you go too far—" Lady Stockton began, but broke off when she saw Rosalind had started to laugh uproariously.

"Oh, Mama, don't mind Judith," Rosalind said as she wiped a tear from her eye. "She's probably speaking the truth anyway, for I don't believe she will be so particular as I have been. And who's to say that she is not right?"

"We'll soon find out, won't we?" Lady Stockton said, then looked thoughtful. "George Cleary has paid you quite a lot of attention this last month. I wonder if he could be serious?"

But Rosalind shook her head. "I'm sure he's not. I've always got along well with Peter's friends, but they've no more ideas about asking me to marry them than I have of accepting them."

"I'm not so sure about that—or at least as far as George is concerned. He's been here quite a number of times now when he knew quite well that Peter was away for the day," Lady Stockton said with a knowing smile.

Rosalind had noticed this, also, but had decided that he must be lonely without any family in town. Should he continue to call so often now that Lady Cleary was in town, then she must try to discourage him kindly, for she knew she could like him only as a friend. He could never make her feel so exhilarated and alive, as "the stranger" in the conservatory had done even before he had kissed her.

The following day, Rosalind found it most interesting to see how Judith's excitement mounted as the day went along, for she herself had experienced no such feelings before her own first visit to Almack's, but had, in fact, been extremely nervous. What Judith would be like on the day of her presentation at court, or her come-out ball, Rosalind could not imagine.

Peter was dressed and waiting in the drawing room when she finally decided to leave her over-eager sister in her mama's capable hands. Taking a good look at him, wearing the court dress which was de rigueur for gentlemen attending Almack's, she decided that he must surely be the most handsome man there this evening. And she wondered how many neckcloths he had wasted before achieving such perfection. A tricorn hat, no longer worn on the head but folded and tucked under one arm, had been placed on the sideboard ready to take with him.

She dropped into a chair and gratefully accepted the glass of sherry he handed to her.

"Is Judith making even more of a fuss than usual?" he asked sympathetically.

"Tonight she can be forgiven, I think," Rosalind told him, "for she has waited for this evening for what seems to all of us to be an absolute age."

"I was away when you had your come-out," he said, smiling. "Were you like this?"

Rosalind shook her head. "I think I was more scared than anything, and trying hard not to show it. We'll keep an eye on her this evening and make sure she has as wonderful a time as she hopes for."

He nodded. "I have a half dozen or more of my friends ready to step in at once if she is without a partner for a single dance, except the waltz, of course."

"I hope they will help me out also, for I'm a little old now for this kind of thing, you know," she said, smiling ruefully, but knowing they would, without asking.

"They have always looked after you, ever since they found out that you were the best of fellows. But you're not worried about partners, surely?" he asked, for she was one of the best dancers he knew, and her card was always filled.

"No, to be honest I'm more concerned about what the pa-

tronesses have to say. Can't you just see Mrs. Drummond
Burrell looking down her nose at me in distaste and saying
nothing, while Sally Jersey will probably open her mouth and,
completely without thinking, say, "You here *again,* Rosalind?"

At the sound of their mama and sister coming down the stairs
Peter went to pour sherry for them, and Rosalind sat up, waiting
to see how her sister finally looked in quite the loveliest gown
she had ever worn.

"Absolutely beautiful," she pronounced when Judith came
into the room. "Your card will be full before the music even
begins, I promise."

"Are you sure?" Judith asked, frowning. "Don't you think
my hair is a little bit too formal?"

Peter went over to her with the sherry. "Not at all. Hetty
surpassed herself and you'll be the envy of all the other young
ladies there," he told her, bending down to kiss her cheek.
"You're going to have a wonderful time."

Two hours later, there was no question but that his prophecy
had been true. Judith's cheeks were flushed and her eyes
sparkled with pleasure as she sat out only for the waltzes and
then had several young men standing near to keep her company.

When they had first arrived, Rosalind found herself eyeing
the young men to see who might be suitable for Judith. There
were a number she knew from previous Seasons who had come
to look over this year's crop, and she looked at them with distaste
when she heard them discussing the merits of the young girls
as though they were cattle ready for the market. She would not
wish her sister to have to dance with any of them, but it soon
appeared that there would be no need, for Judith's card was
quickly filled.

She turned slightly, so that she might discreetly look at her
own card to see who she was dancing with next, and as she
did so she caught a glimpse of a pair of broad shoulders that
seemed more than a little familiar. It must be someone else,
of course, she told herself, for how could she possibly
remember, after what was now more than a year, what anyone
she had seen only once, looked like.

"Why are you frowning?" Peter asked quietly. "Have you seen someone you'd rather not know, for if so I am more than capable of protecting you."

"Of course not, Peter," Rosalind said, forcing a smile and striving to appear normal. "The large man who is with Sally Jersey looked familiar for a moment, that is all."

"I don't believe I've seen him before, but I recognized the name just now when Sally introduced him to Jane Covington. It's Timothy Graystone, and you haven't met him because he has been on the Peninsula for the last few Seasons," he explained. "Do you want to meet him?"

Rosalind was about to say that she was not sure, when the gentleman turned around and she saw that she had been mistaken. It was not "the stranger," as she had begun to call the man she had met under such unusual circumstances in Belvoir Castle, though he was like him enough to be a brother. This gentleman seemed somewhat younger, she decided, but they were so very similar in looks that they must be related.

Because the music began then, Rosalind did not get the opportunity to tell Peter how very much she did want to meet the gentleman, and for the next hour she drifted around the room with different partners who she did not really see at all, though she murmured acceptable phrases which by now she knew by heart. She was, of course, reliving that afternoon in the conservatory.

Between dances, she must have been staring at Lord Graystone without realizing she was doing so, for he smiled at her and made a slight bow and, completely without thinking, Rosalind smiled back. A few minutes later, one of Peter's friends brought him over and made the introductions.

Now Rosalind was flustered and glad that her mama was not near enough to see what had occurred. In trying to rectify things, however, she succeeded only in making matters worse.

"I do beg your pardon, sir," she said, her cheeks taking on a rosy hue. "I know I was staring at you, but it was because you reminded me of someone I met a long time ago."

"I do hope that the memory was a pleasant one," Graystone murmured, smiling. "May I inquire the name of the gentleman who obviously made such an impression upon you?"

If she was flustered before, Rosalind was now even more discomposed. "I'm afraid that I never knew his name," she began, before she realized how ridiculous it sounded. "What I mean is, we were introduced, and . . ."

The bright blue eyes twinkled at her with amusement in exactly the same way as had "the stranger's," so long ago. But this only added to her confusion, and she was much relieved when he took pity on her.

"Before someone comes to claim you," he said quickly, as sets were being formed for a quadrille, "would you by any chance still have a dance open for me?"

Wordlessly, she handed him her card, and he swiftly penciled his name in the last two available, before an old friend of Peter's came to claim her.

Much to her partner's amusement, she stumbled over his feet twice, before recovering her composure and dancing with her usual graceful ease.

"What on earth did that fellow say to you to make you so confused, my dear Rosalind?" he asked. "Would you like me to call him out?"

Rosalind laughed lightly. "Dear me, no, or the poor man will think we're a bunch of complete fools. I was simply embarrassed because every time I tried to say a word to him, something quite idiotic came out. I can't think why, for I am not usually at a loss for words," she said.

"Am I to assume that you do not know him very well?" the young man asked, somewhat puzzled.

"No, and if you see me fall flat on my face when I try to dance with him, you'll know that it is not just my tongue that is tied in knots." Rosalind said, smiling at her own foolishness. "He seems to be a perfectly nice gentleman who has been fighting on the Peninsula for a number of years, so he probably knows very few people in town."

When Graystone's dance came round, he was beside her

quickly, before she could change her mind, but by this time she had recovered her usual equanimity.

"I understand that you have been away in the wars, which is why we have not had the pleasure of your presence here before," she said, as they started to dance.

He inclined his head, smiling politely. "Then this is not your first Season, I assume," he remarked, and when she nodded, he went on, "I know it is not at all the thing for me to suggest, my dear, but it did seem, from your glances, that you wanted to meet me. You have piqued my curiosity, and I cannot help wondering who it could be that I remind you of, for you do not seem to be at all the kind of young lady who would behave indiscreetly with someone whose name she did not even know."

"I am afraid that you are laboring under a misapprehension, my lord," Rosalind said, determinedly keeping a fixed smile on her face, "which I must admit my own confusion has caused. I was once introduced to a gentleman who looked a great deal like you but seemed somewhat older, and I'm afraid that I immediately forgot his name. I have a most dreadful memory for names, and felt too embarrassed at the time to ask for it to be repeated.

"As I was trying to bring the name to mind this evening, I did not realize that I was staring at you. I do not, as a rule, stare at strange gentlemen in such a way, and I am only glad that no one else appears to have noticed. You will, I hope, forgive me?"

"After such a lengthy explanation, how could I not?" Graystone asked. "And now I would suggest we make a fresh start. You have already told me that this is not your first Season, and I would have assumed as much, for you have a more confident air than the young ladies here for the first time."

She smiled at that, and said, "Except, of course, when I trip over my own tongue—a rare occurrence these days, I can assure you."

As the figures of the dance separated them for a few moments, Rosalind could not help feeling that he was right, it was best to forget her awkwardness and start again.

They came together once more, and this time he complimented her prettily upon her grace and proficiency, and before the dance ended she realized he was a most pleasant gentleman, if not exactly the one person she would have liked him to be.

She did not see him at supper, for the dance before the intermission was one of those that George Cleary had chosen, and as Lady Cleary was with her mama, Peter with a young lady she already knew, and Judith with one of Peter's friends, they made up a lively supper party.

Lord Graystone's second dance was a waltz, so that this time there was more opportunity for conversation, and she took advantage of it to find out more about him.

"Were you in the army for long?" she asked him, trying to sound as casual as possible.

"All through the Peninsular campaigns," he told her, "which probably seemed longer to my mama than it did to me. I was one of the lucky ones, however, for throughout the whole campaign I received nothing more than superficial wounds."

"You must have been of grave concern to her, even so," Rosalind murmured, "especially if you are an only child."

"But I am not. I do have an older brother," he told her, "and as he was also over there, I was simply one more for our mama to worry about." He noticed her puzzled frown. "Christopher is a half brother, actually, by my mama's first marriage."

"Oh," she said thoughtfully, for this seemed to her to complicate matters, but if his brother had also been in the wars at the time, he could not be the man she had met.

She changed the subject then, for the last thing she wished was for him to realize just where her questions were leading, and he did not seem to be at all lacking in intelligence.

"You appeared to be with a very large party at supper," he remarked. "I met your mama when I came for the dance, and I assumed that the young lady with you was your sister. Your brother was introduced to me earlier, doubtless at his request so that he could be sure I passed muster."

She grinned and explained. "We've always been very close

and, with my father not yet in town, he feels extremely responsible.''

"Do you think he would mind if I call on you tomorrow afternoon and take you for a drive?" he asked. "That is, of course, if you are not otherwise engaged.''

"I am not, and some fresh air tomorrow afternoon would be delightful,'' she told him, thinking what an excellent opportunity it would be to find out about any male cousins he might have, as well as his mysterious brother.

She was fully aware of the possibility that she might meet "the stranger'' now, and wonder what on earth she had found so fascinating about him. But if she was coming close to seeing him again, she knew that she simply had to take that chance.

When the next afternoon arrived, however, she realized that she was also taking the chance of catching her death of cold, for though the sky was clear and the sun shone brightly, it gave off not the slightest warmth.

"You'd best wrap up well, for it will be cold in an open carriage, and you cannot ride alone with a stranger in a closed carriage,'' her mama warned.

"Lord Graystone seemed to be extremely proper, Mama, and I'm sure he would not even consider breaking any of the rules,'' Rosalind assured her.

When she came down the stairs in her warm, fur-lined cloak and hood, with her hands tucked firmly into a large fur muff, Lady Stockton nodded in satisfaction.

A few minutes later, Lord Graystone rang the doorbell and was shown into the drawing room. He, too, was well wrapped up against the cold.

"I must thank you, my lady, for allowing me to take your daughter for a drive,'' he said, "and I assure you that I will take the greatest care of her.''

Lady Stockton was charmed by his excellent manners, and when they left, a few minutes later, she felt no further qualms as to Rosalind's safety.

Chapter Five

Lord Graystone had been most attentive during the drive in the park. After teasing Rosalind about being dressed as though for a trip to the North Pole, he had produced a furry throw to cover their legs and, wrapped up so very well, the drive had proved delightfully invigorating. If Rosalind's nose closely resembled a cherry before they returned, he had at least refrained from commenting upon it, and she had promised to go for another drive with him again in a few days' time.

But what had pleased Rosalind most was that she had found out, by what she was sure had seemed no more than casual questioning, that his brother, Christopher, had political aspirations and was presently in residence at Holland House where he worked as secretary to Lord Holland.

The very next morning, while Lady Stockton and Judith went once more to the modiste, this time for a fitting of the presentation gown, Rosalind took Hetty with her on a shopping expedition. She had carefully watched how Peter dealt with hackney drivers, and now she hired one herself to take them to Kensington Gardens, alighted at a spot close to Holland House, and paid him off.

By the most fortunate coincidence, just as they strolled past the imposing residence, Christophere Ferguson happened to be returning from an errand and so they came suddenly face to face. Hetty dropped behind at once.

Rosalind's smile was hesitant, for she feared he might not recognize her after so long a time, but when he paused, then came toward her with hands outstretched and a warm smile, her relief knew no bounds.

"My dear," he said softly, disbelief in his face, "I had thought that I would never find you again. I did make discreet inquiries, but dared not be too obvious for fear of damaging your good name."

"I tried also, but as I did not even know your name, it was to no avail until just the other evening," she murmured, "so let me tell you quickly that I am Rosalind Marshall, daughter of Viscount and Lady Stockton, and our home in the country is not far from Belvoir Castle. We are in town for the Season, at Number Six Upper Brook Street."

He looked rather surprised, and then somewhat disappointed. "Christopher Ferguson at your service," he said with a bow, adding gallantly, "but surely by this time you must be promised to someone, if not yet formally affianced."

Rosalind shook her head. "I have not found anyone with whom I would wish to spend the rest of my life," she said quietly, for she had no intention of giving her maid the chance to repeat what she heard. "I came here today to see where you worked, though I did not know if it really was you. It never occurred to me, however, that I might actually meet you like this."

The admission that the meeting was not quite accidental brought a tinge of color to her cheeks.

He raised an eyebrow. "You already knew that I worked for Lord Holland, but did not know if it was me?"

"Lord Graystone told me just yesterday that he had a brother," she explained. "I saw him at Almack's and at first thought that it was you, then I knew it was not, but that you must be closely related to be so alike."

"So you've met Timothy, have you? He's one of the finest fellows in the country," he told her. "Much better than I."

"That is surely a matter of opinion," she murmured. "Could we, perhaps, sit in Kensington Gardens for a few minutes? It's been such a long time since we were together."

"Of course," he readily agreed, then escorted her inside the Gardens and seated her upon a bench. Hetty followed, but at a respectful distance behind.

Rosalind knew that it was not, of course, the thing to do, but there was little chance of their being observed. Members of the *ton* seldom visited Kensington Gardens on an afternoon, and almost never on a morning, for the Gardens had now been taken over by mostly cits and commoners.

Just seeing him again had brought a soft flush to her cheeks and given her a wonderful feeling of well-being. Surely if he, too, had searched for her, he must feel the way she did.

"How did you come to be at the little Marquess's christening if you were, as your brother told me, in the army at the time?" she asked him, for this was something that had puzzled her ever since Lord Graystone had mentioned it.

"I was on leave, recovering from a wound and staying with Lord Holland, who I had known for some time. It was he who brought me to the christening," he said, smiling a little at her curiosity.

"Oh," she said then, remembering that she had never, until this day, actually seen him walking. "Was it a leg injury?"

"A slight one," he said. "Nothing much to worry about, but there was a lull in the fighting and Wellington sent me home to recuperate."

She knew that she should go, and let him return to his work, but now that she had found him again she felt a reluctance to leave without making some arrangement to see him once more. Though she had never been missish, she was not usually forward either, and when he made no effort to suggest another meeting, she decided she must forget her pride.

"Would you like to meet me here again?" she asked hesitantly.

"I would like to do so much more than you can ever imagine," he told her gently, "but I will not meet you without your father's permission, and I do not believe for a moment that he would give it. He must, surely, intend you to marry a man of rank, and I am simply the son of a Scottish cit. Clandestine meetings can cause severe repercussions, you know, for it is only too easy for a lady's reputation to be damaged.''

His reasoning was undoubtedly logical, but Rosalind now felt only the deepest embarrassment at having asked him—and then been turned down. ''What you really mean is that you have no wish to see me again, isn't it?'' she asked, too upset to even try to put it more delicately.

He shook his head sadly. ''No, that is not what I mean, nor is it what I said. But there is so little I am able to offer you at this time, my dear.''

She heard the sorrow in his voice, but was much too hurt herself to pay attention to it. She did, however, listen as he tried to explain.

''Something very special happened to us at Belvoir Castle, and I will never forget or deny it. I only wish that you had been the vicar's daughter, or a member of the family, as I thought you were. I did go there, you know, giving an excuse but really looking for you, and was very well received, but I came away most disappointed. Don't you see that I cannot offer you either a title or the kind of life my brother, or any number of young men about town can. I am by no means a poor man, but I have no town house or country estate such as the one you are so obviously accustomed to.''

Rosalind stood up and faced him, her head held high. Christopher rose also.

''I did not ask you for anything except to meet me again. But as you do not wish to do so, then I'd better go now,'' she said, turning quickly away, for she was very close to tears.

Signaling for her maid to catch up with her, she hurried to where she had seen a hackney rank, stepped into the first carriage in line, and, after telling the driver where to set them down, spoke not a word all the way home.

Christopher's eyes were sad as he watched her go, now quite sure that he would never see her again. He had hated to see the joy in her face change to sorrow, but to have tried to make her understand his feelings would only have caused her more unhappiness in the end. At least, now he could find out how she was going along from his brother.

With a sigh, he walked slowly out of the Gardens and over to Holland House. Right now, his work would be the best cure for what ailed him, if any cure was possible.

His position as secretary to Lord Holland was, in essence, a means to an end. It was an excellent training ground for what he eventually hoped to achieve, which was first a seat in the House and, ultimately, if he could prove himself worthy of it, a Cabinet post. Lord Holland was aware of this, and willing to help him in every possible way.

As he had told Rosalind, he was not without funds, for his father had been already well established at the time he had married his mama, and at his death he had left quite a substantial sum of money, well invested. A self-made businessman, he had been highly respected in Edinburgh and, though not titled, could easily have bought one for himself if such a thing had appealed to him.

And he might possibly have done so, more for his wife's sake than his own, had he lived longer, but he had died suddenly when Christopher was only two years old, leaving a portion of his estate to his widow, and the balance in trust for his little son.

The Earl of Glastonbury had met the widow, who came from a titled Scottish family, just after her husband died, and two years later she consented to become his countess provided he would also take care of her young son. He had readily agreed, and when Christopher was five, to his untold joy, his half brother had been born, and they had been the best of friends ever since.

Lady Stockton was delighted that Rosalind had taken an interest in someone at last. She liked Lord Graystone very much, and soon both he and George Cleary seemed to be always underfoot. They did, of course, pay attention to both of her girls, for they were gentlemen and would not have dreamed of breaking their unwritten rules. She had a strong feeling, however, that Rosalind's preference was for the young viscount.

She frequently wrote long letters to Lord Stockton, and had regular but brief replies from him, but so far he had made no mention of when he might come to town. What would happen if one of the gentlemen was nearing a proposal and her husband was not in town to receive it? she wondered.

Instead of continuing to tease herself in this way, Lady Stockton decided to inform her husband, in her next letter, that she was quite sure one of Rosalind's admirers was about to come up to scratch and make her an offer of marriage, and that he must come to town as soon as possible to receive it. If he came at once, she thought to herself, it would also give her time to see that he had all the right clothes with him for Judith's presentation, now only two weeks away.

Being a good, affectionate father, when he received the letter he set out for London at once, but, unfortunately, Lady Stockton was out on the morning he arrived, and only Rosalind was at home. They met in the hall, and he took her arm and led her immediately into his study.

"Well, my dear," he began, after giving her a warm hug, "I understand that you've been seeing a great deal of a certain gentleman, and that he's about to make you an offer. I'm delighted, of course, for though your mama and I are not anxious to lose you, we have always wanted you to marry and be as happy as we are."

Rosalind regarded him in complete amazement. "What can you possibly be talking about, Papa?" she asked. "I have been seeing several gentlemen, but I have not the least intention of marrying any of them. I'm afraid that you must have misunderstood Mama."

Lord Stockton had, with great reluctance, left his estates in the complete charge of his bailiff, who was a capable enough man but only when properly supervised. Given another week, he could have come to town with an easy mind, but his wife had indicated that the matter was urgent. Now this daughter, who had turned down more offers than he could count on both hands, was telling him that there was no reason for him to be here.

It was most fortunate for Rosalind that Lady Stockton returned just then and was told immediately that her husband was here in his study. Never dreaming that either Rosalind or anyone else might be with him, she hastened into the study without pausing to remove either her bonnet or her pelisse.

"Geoffrey, my dear, how good of you to come so soon," she said, hurrying over to him with outstretched arms. "Had I but known, I'd not have been out when you arrived, I promise."

"We are not alone, my dear," he said, coolly, putting aside her arms and giving her a small peck on her cheek.

She swung around at once, to find Rosalind standing only five feet away, with an expression on her face that could only be described as mutinous.

"Your arrival was most opportune, my dear," Lord Stockton said in a dangerously quiet voice. "I came post haste when I got your letter, only to find that, according to Rosalind, she is not seeing any particular gentleman, and is no nearer to thinking of marriage than she ever was. I might add that I left my bailiff in charge at a crucial time, and there is a distinct possibility that he will ruin every bit of the work I have done this year."

"Whatever Rosalind says, she has two suitors vying with each other, and I know that one or both of them will propose marriage at any moment," Lady Stockton said, firmly defending her actions. "They are most eminently suitable, and two of the most delightful young men you could wish for. One is George Cleary, who you will recall came into the earldom when his papa died, and the other is Viscount Timothy Graystone, Glastonbury's heir."

"They are both very good friends of Peter and Judith, as well as myself," Rosalind insisted, now extremely upset. "And there has been no talk of marriage from either one of them. Why do you always spoil everything, Mama? I was enjoying their friend-ship very much, and now you have turned it into something it certainly was not.''

''If you refuse both of these gentlemen, Rosalind,'' Lady Stockton said sternly, ''I can assure you that it will finally scare off everyone else. You will become known as the Ice Maiden, make us all the laughing stock of the *ton,* and completely ruin Judith's first Season. If your papa has any sense of responsibility, he will insist that you accept the first one of these gentlemen who proposes, and make you behave like any normal child of mine would if she was capable of even the slightest consideration for the feelings of others.''

Completely shocked by her mama's words, Rosalind glanced from one to the other of them with a look of horror in her eyes, then she ran from the room.

Lord Stockton glanced at his wife, a sorrowful expression on his face, for he could not bring himself to scold her. He went over and closed the door that Rosalind had left open, then he said quietly, ''I am very sorry that you went so far, my dear, for she is only twenty, and I am not as yet prepared to force her into an unhappy marriage. She is a good, warmhearted girl, and I would like her to have the kind of love match we have enjoyed.''

''But she will ruin Judith's chances this year if we're not careful,'' Lady Stockton protested.

''No, she won't,'' he countered, ''for if one of the young men comes to me I will put him off, without saying either yes or no, and they can wait all summer, if necessary, to give Judith her chance. But I cannot apprehend why the most affectionate of our daughters has not yet fallen head over heels in love with a suitable young man.''

Lady Stockton sat down on the sofa and motioned for him to join her, and when he did so she rested her head against his shoulder for a moment before saying, ''I've had the feeling for some time now that Rosalind did once meet someone and fell in love more than a year ago. She has never mentioned a word to me about it, but you recall all the pomp and ceremony surrounding the little Marquess of Granby's christening?''

Lord Stockton nodded. "You think it was then?"

"I don't know how she could have met someone, for to my knowledge she was never out alone," Lady Stockton said, a puzzled expression on her face, "but Rosalind looked to me, for quite a long time, like a girl who had fallen in love. I watched her very carefully, for I was afraid that she might be meeting someone secretly, but am certain that she met no one from the time I began to watch her.

"Gradually the look faded, and she's never been quite the same since, except for just about the time she met Lord Graystone. This is why I sent for you, for I felt sure they were going to make a match of it.''

He reached out and took her hand in his. "Leave it alone for now, my love. I'll have a word with her, and make sure she realizes that you don't mean what you said, and whether the bailiff makes a mess of things or not, I'll stay on, for Rosalind's happiness is much more important to me than a few acres of land.''

He gently drew her into his arms and at last received the welcome kiss that she had offered before she knew that her daughter was in the room.

A short time later, Lady Stockton went to the kitchens to make sure that a substantial luncheon was being prepared, while her husband went up to Rosalind's bedchamber to have a little talk with his daughter. He wished to reassure her that, for the time being, there would be no pressure brought to bear upon her in the matter of selecting a husband.

Lord Stockton also made a point of being present that same afternoon when Lord Graystone came to call, but to everyone's surprise, particularly Rosalind's, he brought with him a half brother by the name of Christopher Ferguson.

Except for the slight difference in age, they might have been twins, they were so alike, and when Lady Stockton saw Rosalind's face turn pale, and watched her grasp the back of a chair for support, there was no question in her mind as to who this young man was. What she did not understand was what could have happened to keep them apart.

With Lord Stockton present, the gentlemen spent some time discussing Napoleon's escape from Elba, and the reception he was receiving once again from the French people as he slowly made his way through France, gathering supporters and soldiers as he went.

"What do you think will happen?" Lord Stockton asked the two gentlemen who had helped put Napoleon on Elba.

"In my opinion there's no question about it," Christopher Ferguson said. "We'll have to go back, sir, and do the job properly this time. At the rate he is gathering support, he'll have a large army together very soon now, I should think."

Lord Stockton nodded. "Wellington can do little without experienced men, though there'll be a lot of additional bloodshed if it really comes to a battle. How could they have allowed him to escape like that?"

He glanced across at Rosalind who had been listening to their conversation, and noticed how pale she had become.

"Oh dear," Judith wailed, "if all the gentlemen have to go away it will ruin the Season."

"Do you think the battle will be soon, Papa?" Rosalind asked quietly, much more concerned with the loss of men than its effect upon the Season.

"I should think so, at the rate Napoleon is progressing through France," Lord Stockton said. "What do you think, Lord Graystone?"

Instead of answering at once, Graystone turned to his brother with eyebrows raised.

Christopher shook his head. "He's going to slow down as he comes north," he said quietly. "I would say that it will be May at the earliest, for if he's not stopped first—and there's no one at present in a position to stop him—he'll try to gather as big an army as he can before taking us on. That will, of course, be to our advantage, for it will give Wellington time to get an army together again also."

Lord Stockton gave Ferguson a look of respect. "You've got a point there that I hadn't thought of," he said. "But what a tremendous task it will be to get the army together once more when it has been virtually disbanded for almost a year! There'll be many who will no longer fit into their uniforms after returning to a life of leisure."

"Only the officers," Christopher said dryly, "for many of the enlisted men have been starving to death as they searched desperately for work. There's no doubt, though, that Napoleon has a decided advantage, for he's had ten months of exile in which to think over where he went wrong, and what he must do to rectify his mistakes. 'Come and range yourselves under the flags of your leader . . . the eagle and tricolor shall fly from steeple to steeple to the towers of Notre Dame.' That is what he has told the French army, and they are flocking to him."

"You seem to be very well-informed, Ferguson," Lord Stockton said quietly. "Have you some connection with the government?"

"I hope to have eventually, sir, but at present I am merely employed as secretary to Lord Holland," Ferguson told him. "I have no doubt that Napoleon feels the Whigs will restrain the government from making war on him, but he is wrong. We didn't fight him all those years, and lose so many brave men, to let him win now."

"Surely you won't have to take part in a battle with Napoleon?" Judith suggested, turning to Lord Graystone. "Why can't all those ex-soldiers we see on the London streets fight him instead?"

He smiled at her, a little indulgently. "They'll be glad to join us, I'm sure," he told her, "and we'll be thankful indeed, for we need experienced men, but as many officers as are able will go back, including myself, for the soldiers need leaders. But for now, I was wondering if my brother and I could take you young ladies for a ride in the park?"

Rosalind and Judith hurried upstairs to put on pelisses, bonnets, and such, which took no more than a few minutes, then they accepted help into the open carriage and set out toward Park Lane.

It was a lovely, springlike day, and the park was quite crowded with carriages and gentlemen on horseback, taking advantage of the sunshine. By now, both young ladies knew quite a lot of people in town, as did Lord Graystone, so they made frequent stops to pass the time of day.

Lady Jersey's eyes sparkled as she approached and made it clear that she meant to stop.

"My goodness, Lord Graystone, you've most certainly been keeping something from us. This gentleman cannot be anything else but your brother, and what a handsome pair you make," she declared, scenting a mystery.

"Allow me to make known to you my half brother, Christopher Ferguson, my lady," Lord Graystone said, leaning back so that his brother could clasp her hand.

"Ferguson?" Lady Jersey murmured thoughtfully, then asked, "From Edinburgh originally, aren't you? I seem to recall that Lady Graystone had been married before and had a child. Aren't you the young protégé of Lord Holland?"

His blue eyes twinkled as he told her, with a grin, "A hired hand, actually, my lady. I work for him as his secretary."

But Lady Jersey was not to be fobbed off. "I don't doubt that he puts you to work, but as your father was a wealthy businessman, I'd question that you need the funds. I'll send you a voucher for Almack's, for you two young men will be the talk of the town this Season, I'll be bound."

As Lady Jersey drove on, Christopher looked decidedly embarrassed, and Rosalind did not help matters by giving him a most decidedly gleeful look.

"I knew this was a mistake," he said quietly to his brother. "But you need not give it a thought, for I've no particular desire to go to Almack's."

"But you must go!" Judith declared in such a loud voice that Rosalind gave her a nudge. She turned and glared at her older sister, then caught Lord Graystone's eye and subsided at once.

"We'll talk about it later," Lord Graystone said quietly to

his brother, then turned to Rosalind. "Isn't that George Cleary over there, my dear?"

"Yes," Rosalind said, glancing in the direction he had indicated, "but he's not seen us for he's going in the direction of Park Lane. He's with his mama, Lady Cleary, and is probably on his way to visit our house, for word has probably reached them that Papa is now in town."

She had a sudden, acute feeling of misgiving. Despite the pleasant conversation with her father, which had reassured her for the time being in regard to the way he meant to treat any of her suitors, she could not help but be concerned in case George had decided it was time he came up to scratch. If she was right, and Papa was to succeed in what he meant to do, it would be best if they stayed out a little longer.

"Why don't we take another turn around," she suggested brightly. "It's such a beautiful afternoon that I feel we should take advantage of the weather while we can."

She looked up and caught Christopher's eyes upon her, and was furious with herself when her limbs seemed to turn to jelly. He obviously didn't want her, so why must he make her feel this way?

Then she realized that his expression held nothing but tenderness, and the jelly started melting. Lord Graystone was in a deep conversation with her sister, and so she allowed herself to smile very faintly at Christopher.

"Am I forgiven for hurting you so?" he asked her quietly.

She shook her head, then murmured, "I'm not sure, nor do I know that my mama quite approves of you."

"Then we'll just have to wait and see what both your parents decide as to my antecedents. I'm sure they will have discussed them," he told her, "for your mama asked me a lot of leading questions just before we started talking with Lord Stockton about Napoleon's escape."

By the time they had circled the park once more, and had stopped to speak to several more of their friends, the sun had gone in and a cool wind had started to blow.

"I think we'd best take you ladies home," Lord Graystone

said quietly, "for I'd not like to be the cause of either of you catching the slightest chill. It has been a most interesting afternoon, however."

Rosalind silently agreed for, aside from Lady Jersey's remarks, she had not failed to notice how very many ladies of the *ton* had cast envious glances their way. When the brothers were together they certainly made a very striking pair. It was a little disconcerting, however, when the gentlemen were the ones who drew attention rather than the ladies.

Chapter Six

"I must say that the two young men look as like as two peas in a pod except, perhaps, for a slight difference in years," Lady Stockton remarked when her daughters had discarded their outer wear and joined her for a cup of tea in the drawing room.

"Oh, Mama, it was the most intriguing thing to see the way everyone turned to look at them, particularly the ladies," Judith said. "And absolutely everybody who is anybody either waved or stopped to speak with us."

"I am not at all surprised," her mama stated, with a rather doubtful expression on her face. "And did you say that Sally Jersey insisted that the elder brother, Mr. Ferguson, be admitted to Almack's?"

"She said she was going to send him a voucher, though he did not ask her for one. I heard her quite distinctly," Judith avowed, "so he must be completely acceptable even though he does not have a title."

"Oh dear, I quite forgot. Didn't you say that you had to write a note to your friend, Caroline, my dear?" Lady Stockton asked her, appearing suddenly worried. "If you'd like to do it now, before you dress for dinner, I'll excuse you so that it will not make you late."

Judith jumped up quickly. "Oh, thank you, Mama," she said,

"I had completely forgotten about it, and she would have been so cross."

As soon as she had left the drawing room, Lady Stockton walked over to the door and closed it firmly. Rosalind's eyebrows rose questioningly, for this was most unusual.

"I am somewhat concerned as to who Mr. Ferguson is," Lady Stockton said quietly, carefully watching her daughter's face as she spoke, "for I experienced the strangest feeling this afternoon that this was not the first time you had met him."

Rosalind looked decidedly embarrassed, for she had not for a moment realized that she had given herself away. "I did meet him once, a long time ago," she admitted rather truculently.

"I do not recall your having mentioned his name," her mama remarked coldly, "but in that case I am sure you will be able to tell me exactly what his relationship to Lord Graystone is."

"He is his half brother, as I believe Lord Graystone did say," Rosalind reminded her. When her mama said nothing further, she added, a little defensively, "He was the countess's first child, by her former husband, a Scot by the name of Mr. Ferguson."

"And have you any idea who this Mr. Ferguson was, for surely he was already deceased when she married the Earl of Glastonbury, or there would have been the most dreadful scandal," Lady Stockton asked, determinedly persistent until she got to the bottom of this.

Rosalind shifted uncomfortably. She simply could not understand why her mama would not accept him if Lady Jersey had done so, and she finally turned angrily toward Lady Stockton and said sharply, "He was an Edinburgh businessman of some sort. You would call him a cit, I suppose, for he made a lot of money and then died when Christopher was two years old."

Her mama sighed heavily, for it was more than obvious that Rosalind had not found this out during the course of a carriage ride in the park. If she had, then Judith would have been absolutely full of it and more than eager to impart the information.

"How long have you been on a first-name basis?" she asked

her daughter. "I do not recall hearing you ever speak so familiarly of Lord Graystone or Lord Cleary, or do you, perhaps, do so in private?"

Rosalind rose quickly. "No, I do not," she snapped, "and I do not address Mr. Ferguson as Christopher, either. You can always ask Judith, as you usually do in any case. And now I'd best go and change, for my sister will be up in the boughs if I keep Hetty too long."

Moving swiftly, she was out of the room almost before she finished speaking, leaving Lady Stockton to sit alone, sipping her tea and wondering what could have taken place at that first meeting a long time ago—but, unfortunately, not long enough for her daughter to have forgotten this undoubtedly good-looking and intelligent young man.

Had it been one of the other patronesses who had offered Mr. Ferguson a voucher, Lady Stockton would have felt much more assured that his eligibility had been thoroughly checked out, but Sally Jersey was a little inclined to go too much by her own instincts. However, he was the son of a countess, which surely must mean something, and he had to have been brought up by the earl.

Why could not Rosalind have fallen in love with Lord Graystone? she asked herself. He had just the same looks, without all those confusing problems about his birth, and there was not the least doubt that one day he would be an earl.

It was with some relief that she heard her husband enter the house, and a few minutes later he joined her in the drawing room.

"Now, my dear," he said jovially, "what can have got you into such a gloomy frame of mind? If it's that young man who works for Lord Holland, I must tell you that I was most impressed with him, and there was no doubt at all that Lord Graystone deferred to his opinion."

"But he's the son of a Scottish cit, Geoffrey," Lady Stockton protested. "Rosalind told me that much, and she did meet him some time ago, just as I thought."

"Well, let's hope he was a wealthy cit, and left the young

fellow comfortably off," Lord Stockton said with a grin. "Seemed to me that he had a good head on his shoulders for his age, and I'd not at all mind having him for a son-in-law, if that's how they both feel."

"I'd like us to get to know a lot more about him before that kind of decision is made," his wife asserted, most disappointed that he, also, was quite prepared to accept the young man purely on his face value. "Can you believe that Sally Jersey is sending him a voucher to Almack's just on the basis of meeting him in the park? I only wish it had been one of the other patronesses, for they would have thoroughly checked that young man out first."

"Sally is no one's fool, even if she does talk a little too much sometimes, and don't forget that she is a friend of the Hollands," Lord Stockton informed her. "Let's not jump to a lot of conclusions before we've even found out if the two of them are at all interested in each other. It's soon enough for me to check on him when and if he asks me for her hand."

"Do you mean that you would not object to our daughter marrying a Whig? I'm not at all sure that I would like the idea, and you know that he must be one if he's working for Holland," his wife declared, then she looked thoughtful. "It has just occurred to me where they must have met, for Lord Holland did attend the little Marquess of Granby's christening, didn't he? I'll warrant he must have brought Mr. Ferguson with him."

"Wasn't Rosalind supposed to be at your side the whole time, my dear?" Lord Stockton suggested slyly. "Or do you not, perhaps, recall?"

"Both girls were at my side all the time," she snapped, "except for when they went to join a party that was being shown around the castle by the duchess. I did suspect, though, that Judith really wanted to be with her friend, Mary Goodwin, but I knew they'd be safe enough with Charlotte Goodwin, for she always keeps an eye on the girls." She glanced up at him as a thought came to her. "Do you suppose that Rosalind wandered off somewhere on her own?"

"I'd not be at all surprised to find out that she did so," Lord Stockton said, "and you should have known, my dear, that she might, but it seems to me to be rather late now for recriminations."

Lady Stockton had little option but to agree at that time, but when, several days later, a note came from Lady Holland inviting them all to dinner some two weeks hence, she immediately became alarmed.

Her son, Peter, was with her in the morning room when she opened the envelope, and he turned to her in surprise when she said, quite loudly, "Oh, no, we can't possibly accept such an invitation."

"Then do not do so, Mama," he suggested cheerfully. "You can always say you have another engagement on that evening, can't you? Who is it from, anyway?"

"It's from Lord and Lady Holland, and they are inviting all of us to attend an informal dinner in two weeks' time," she moaned. "This has to be Rosalind's doing and I must have a word with her at once."

Peter frowned. "How does Rosalind know the Hollands?" he asked, puzzled.

"I don't believe that she does," Lady Stockton told him, "but, with the exception of yourself, we have all met Lord Graystone's brother, Mr. Ferguson, and it is my understanding that he is Lord Holland's secretary. I suppose that must be the reason why we have received the invitation."

"It would seem that Mr. Ferguson is rather more than a secretary if the Hollands have asked us because of his connection," Peter remarked astutely. "But I, for one, would be very interested to go, for I have heard that they have the most unusual dinner parties."

"Dinner parties suitable for your two sisters to attend?" Lady Stockton asked dryly.

"I believe the guests are usually less . . . conspicuous . . . than their hostess," Peter said, looking somewhat embarrassed. "Lord Holland is accepted everywhere, but Lady Holland is not acknowledged by some high sticklers of the *ton*, which is grossly unfair, of course, for if one party was guilty, then so was the other.''

"I cannot help but agree that it should not be so, but as you well know by now, Peter, there has always been one standard for gentlemen and quite another for ladies," Lady Stockton declared.

Her son shrugged, acknowledging the obvious, then he looked puzzled. "But I still cannot see what connection the Hollands have with Rosalind," he observed.

"Oh dear," his mama said with a sigh. "I keep forgetting that you were away when Lord Graystone called and brought his half brother with him. They are uncannily alike in looks, though Mr. Christopher Ferguson is indubitably the older. It appears that Rosalind met him once, more than a year ago, and though I cannot think why, she seems to be a great deal more interested in him than in Lord Graystone."

"I see," Peter mused. "I really missed something by going off to the races for a few days, didn't I? It would seem that you are not very pleased with Rosalind's taste in brothers, but how about Papa? Does he feel the same way as you obviously do?"

Lady Stockton shrugged expressively. "I don't dislike Mr. Ferguson, but the younger brother would, of course, be the more suitable for he is the only son of an earl. However, your papa was much impressed with Mr. Ferguson's ideas when they started to discuss Napoleon's escape from Elba. He thought him to be most intelligent and well informed."

"I see," Peter said with a grin. "Then I'm sure he will wish to accept the invitation, but I hope that, in the meantime, I will have a chance to meet this Mr. Ferguson, for I am more than a little interested in seeing for myself a gentleman who has finally captured my sister Rosalind's interest."

His wish was granted that very afternoon, for the brothers arrived together, as before. Peter was in the drawing room when they were announced.

"So you are the mysterious Mr. Ferguson I have been hearing so much about," Peter murmured, smiling a little grimly as they shook hands.

Christopher looked at him inquiringly and waited for him to elaborate on his statement.

"My mama seems to think that you met my sister some time ago under somewhat mysterious circumstances," Peter said, then paused to see what Ferguson's reaction might be.

"Does she? And what does your sister have to say in the matter?" Christopher asked, smiling imperturbably.

"As a matter of fact, I haven't asked her," Peter admitted. "She seems to be a bit edgy right now, so I thought it best not to approach her."

"A very sensible decision, I would say," Christopher said, still smiling. "I'm sure she'll tell you all about it when she feels the time is right. Ah, here she is now, but I'd wait a while to ask her questions if I were you."

He turned to greet Rosalind and Judith, then listened while his brother, who had been conversing with Lady Stockton, suggested that the two young ladies might enjoy a ride in the park again.

Fifteen minutes later the four of them stepped into the open carriage and set out in the direction of the park, but just as they entered, Lord Graystone suggested they take a different direction from the usual one. Shortly thereafter, they found themselves in a much quieter part.

"I thought that perhaps you two might need some time alone," he said quietly to his brother and Rosalind, "for I do not believe that a single word has passed between you since we left the house."

Christopher looked closely at Rosalind's hesitant expression and then assured her, "I promise you'll come to no harm, my dear, and I would like to have about fifteen minutes alone with you, if I may."

"Very well," Rosalind said, "but Judith, you'll not tell Mama, will you?"

Judith shook her head, quite happy to agree, for it would mean that she would be alone with Lord Graystone, something she had looked forward to for some time.

Christopher jumped quickly down, then gave his hand to Rosalind to assist her, and as soon as they reached the footpath, the carriage drew away.

Christopher took Rosalind's arm and led her along a smaller path between some trees, and a moment later they came to a bench. Taking out a handkerchief, Christopher carefully wiped the surface so that Rosalind's gown might not be stained, then she sat down a little gingerly, and he settled close by.

This was the first time that they had been absolutely alone since the rendezvous in Kensington Gardens when he had refused to arrange a clandestine meeting with her, and she had returned home completely heartsick. Rosalind meant to make the most of this opportunity, but first there were some questions to be answered, and she looked away for a moment, trying to decide where to begin.

"I thought I was never going to be able to get you alone again," Christopher murmured in her ear.

She turned to face him, her eyes clearly angry, for she had still not forgiven him for the hurt he had inflicted when they had been in Kensington Gardens.

"I think you owe me an explanation, sir, for your apparent change of heart. Was it, perhaps, because you found out that your brother was also showing some interest in me?" she asked.

He shook his head. "I would never behave in such a fashion, as I am sure you must realize," he told her, a little sternly. "After our meeting in the Gardens, I found that I could not bear to lose touch with you altogether, so I went to Timothy to ask if he would let me know, from time to time, how you were going along." His eyes held some of the despair he had felt at that moment. "By then, however, he had apparently realized that you must be the mysterious woman for whom I had been searching some twelve months ago. It was at his insistence that I joined him when he next called upon you, so that I could try to find out if you had forgiven me.''

"I did tell you, on that extremely interesting drive in the park, that I had not,'' Rosalind said sharply.

"And still have not, I perceive," Christopher murmured. "Is there no way I can make you understand that I was trying only to protect you and to behave in your best interests, not my own?''

"It hurt too much for me to understand anything," she said, her voice barely a whisper. "I would never have asked anyone else to meet me like that, and when you turned me down I swore I would never again put myself in such a humiliating position.''

"I am so very sorry to have caused you so much pain. I was then, however, and still am, only too aware of my quite lowly position when it comes to the marriage stakes. I was never so surprised in my life as when Lady Jersey offered to send me a voucher for Almack's. It arrived just the other day.'' He held her hand in his two large ones and waited for some response.

"I've never considered that a title counted for much, for in the last two years and more I've met too many men who didn't deserve to have one," she told him. "Nor do I feel that having a lot of money is so very important. Can we not put that awful meeting behind us and start anew?''

"Of course we can," he agreed gladly. "But I am not going to promise that it will now be all smooth sailing for us. I believe that we both have our share of stubbornness, and this will not be the last time we strongly disagree about something. But, for my part, I wouldn't want you to be any other way.''

"Nor would I wish you to agree with everything I say or do," she told him, with a smile that held more than a trace of mischievousness. "But making up is the very nicest thing of all. However, you must not be led to think that I have agreed to marry you as yet.''

"Of course not," Christopher said with a grin, "nor should you think that I have as yet proposed marriage to you. And I must seriously consider the advisability, for I have the strongest feeling that nothing less than a proposal on bended knee would suffice for you.''

''And your poor knees would possibly never recover?'' she asked with a chuckle.

''How did you guess?'' he asked. ''Or did you, perhaps, hear them creaking as I descended from the coach?''

He rose and reached for her hand to assist her. ''We'd best return to the carriage, or my brother will be wondering what has become of us,'' he said. Then, before releasing the small hand, he turned back her glove and placed a warm, tender kiss upon the inside of her wrist.

They walked side by side until they reached the spot where they had been set down, and almost as once the carriage came into sight.

''Well, at least you look a good deal happier now than when we left you here,'' Lord Graystone remarked, quite obviously pleased with himself.

He had such a pleasant disposition that Rosalind almost wished she could love him instead of his brother, but it was not what fate had decreed, and he would probably have let her have all her own way—something that had never proved very good for her.

As the carriage took them back to the fashionable area of the park, she glanced over at Judith, and she did not fail to notice that her sister seemed not at all displeased with the deviation from the usual ride in the park. She could not help wondering if, perhaps, her sister was becoming not a little interested in Lord Graystone. What a turnabout it would be if they were to eventually make a match of it!

''Won't people think it strange if they saw only two of us in the carriage before, and now there are four?'' she asked Lord Graystone.

''No one saw two people, my dear, for I did not think it wise to start them wondering. We continued along to Oxford Street, then went out of the park and came back along Park Lane,'' he told her.

"That was very thoughtful of you, my lord," Rosalind said quietly, "and I, for one, appreciate it very much."

"It was my pleasure," he replied, "for I must say that I very much enjoyed your sister's company."

Judith's eyes shone and her cheeks took on a rosy hue at his words.

They were now wending their way slowly through the press of fashionable people in carriages and on horseback, stopping as little as possible, but were compelled to do so when they heard the loud voice of Lady Jersey, calling to them to stay where they were as her coachman endeavored to bring her carriage alongside of them.

"You naughty boy," she scolded Christopher when at last she was close by. "I sent you a voucher and then you did not come."

"I do beg your pardon most sincerely, my lady," he said charmingly, reaching across to clasp her hand in his, "but I had a commitment that I could not possibly get out of. I assure you, however, that I do appreciate it, and I will be at the very next Assembly."

Rosalind could not help but be pleased to notice that Lady Jersey was no more able to resist Christopher's charm than she was.

"Very well, you rogue," Lady Jersey said, "I'll forgive you this time, but just make sure you come, for I'll be looking for you."

When they reached Upper Brook Street, it was quite obvious that it was their mama's afternoon for receiving guests to tea. The two gentlemen declined the very pressing invitations to come inside from both Rosalind and Judith, but they did promise to do so on the very next occasion.

After hurrying up the stairs to discard their hats and gloves, they came back to the drawing room. It was fortunate that Peter had stayed home that afternoon, for he was doing his duty quite admirably, taking cups over to be refilled and passing plates of dainty sandwiches and pastries among the guests.

There was a group of young ladies, daughters of some of their mama's friends, who were congregated at one end of the large drawing room, and this was where Judith went right away to make sure they knew who had taken her out that afternoon. Rosalind, however, noticed how tired and harassed her mama looked, and went over to her to see what she could do to help.

"It must be the fine weather that has brought everyone out, for I declare that I have never had so many guests in one single afternoon, and you two both out," Lady Stockton complained. "Just see what you can do to help Peter, will you, my dear?"

But in less than fifteen minutes, just as if someone had blown a whistle, all but two or three of the guests had disappeared, and the ones remaining were Lady Stockton's bosom-bows.

As she joined them, sinking thankfully into a chair, one of her friends asked, "What was that you were trying to tell me, my dear Margaret, about being invited to dine at Holland House? I know she's not considered to be quite the thing, but I'd go in a flash if I were asked."

"Why is she not quite the thing, Mama?" Judith asked, despite Lady Stockton's frowns. "Is she divorced or something?"

"She's divorced *and* something," Lady Charlesworth said with a chuckle. "But I agree with Martha. I'd go just to see what it was like, though I know the high sticklers would not."

"And would you take your daughters?" Lady Stockton asked, "for Peter and my girls have been invited, too."

"I would," the forthright Martha Donaldson said, "for with you and Lord Stockton there, what harm can they come to? And I do hear that her dinner parties are vastly amusing."

"I've no doubt of that," Lady Drake remarked with a little laugh, "but are they really intended to be? How does Lord Stockton feel about it?"

"He declares he wouldn't miss it for anything, for he feels there will be more intelligent conversation there in one evening than he hears in a month," Lady Stockton said a little plaintively, "so I suppose we'll have to accept."

She suddenly realized that both her daughters were listening with a great deal of interest, and, turning to them, said, "Thank you for your help, and if you want to run upstairs now and start getting dressed, I'll excuse you."

With some reluctance, they left the drawing room, but as they went up the stairs Judith asked her sister in a loud whisper, "What do you suppose they meant by 'divorced and something?' "

"I have not the slightest idea," Rosalind said, "and I would not advise you to try asking Mama."

"I'd not dream of doing anything so silly," Judith told her, "for if I did she would be sure to tell me that I must stay home that evening so as not to put her to shame. Now I wouldn't miss going for anything, and there I thought it would be a boring political evening."

Rosalind laughed. "You are growing up quickly, aren't you, little sister? And I did not fail to notice that you did not at all mind being left in the carriage with Lord Graystone this afternoon."

Her sister was serious for a moment. "I like him very much, Ros, far more than any of the gentlemen I have met so far. And I really cannot understand how you can prefer a plain mister over a viscount."

"It's not a case of comparing one person to another, like apples and pears," Rosalind said a little sadly. "I can no more stop loving Christopher than I can stop the sun shining or the moon making its way through the heavens. You'll know what it's like if you ever really feel this way."

"All I can say," Judith declared, "is that I have no wish to feel that way if all it does is make you as unhappy as you have been at times."

Rosalind shrugged. "Then you'll never know what it is to be truly happy, either. But I believe that very soon now everything is going to work out for us. Perhaps Mama will find that she and Lady Holland have many things in common that she would never have believed."

Chapter Seven

The dinner invitation was, of course, accepted despite Lady Stockton's misgivings, and when the family arrived at Holland House, Christopher Ferguson came forward to meet them and to make the necessary introductions. Lord Holland had met Lord Stockton on a number of occasions in the past, as was to be expected, and he greeted his guests most cordially. He was a man who possessed that special quality which immediately sets people at ease, and Rosalind took an instant liking to him.

He was, in fact, so charming to Lady Stockton that she was completely disarmed and fully prepared to enjoy the evening—that is, until she made the acquaintance of her hostess, Lady Holland.

She had heard that the Hollands' dinner table was inclined to be overcrowded, and had thought it a probable exaggeration, and when fourteen guests were to be seated at a table set for twelve but large enough for no more than nine, she naturally assumed that extra leaves would be added. Lady Holland, however, proceeded to order, in the most domineering fashion, that chairs be pushed closer together—quite a feat that caused Lady Stockton's own and both of her daughters' gowns to become inevitably creased.

Seated on Lord Holland's right, she did, however, enjoy his charm and wit, but she could not help glancing over occasionally to where, on the other side of the table, Judith and Rosalind sat, with Christopher Ferguson squashed in between them in the most dreadfully familiar way.

"Have no fears about the young man," Lord Holland said as he noted the direction in which her glance so frequently strayed. "You'll never find a better one for your daughter, I can tell you. He's going to go a long way. That is, of course, if he doesn't get himself killed in this tomfool war that seems to be starting up again."

"Do you think that he really means to go over there to fight, sir?" Lady Stockton asked. "I don't believe my daughter is aware of any such intention on his part, or I am sure she would have mentioned it to me."

"There's no doubt about it. All he's waiting for is to hear from Wellington that they're ready, and he'll be off like a shot," he stated emphatically. "I've tried my best to talk him out of it, but he's a very determined young man when his mind's made up. It must be the Scot in him."

"Now don't you go jawing Lady Stockton's head off, my lord," Lady Holland called loudly across the table. "Give her a chance to talk to Sir Edward Castleton for a while."

Of course, everyone at the table heard her, and most of them paid it no heed, for this was the usual autocratic way in which Lady Holland spoke to her husband and to all her guests. But Rosalind had the most dreadful time trying to keep herself from laughing at the completely shocked expression on her mama's face.

"Do you think that she has taken Mama in dislike?" She murmured the question into Christopher's ear.

"No, my dear, not at all," he said at once. "That's just the way she always speaks to Lord Holland. It has nothing whatever to do with Lady Stockton, believe me."

"I have to admit that she sets a lavish table and each dish is more delicious than the next," Rosalind said quietly, having finally gained control of a dreadful desire to laugh.

Christopher nodded. "Always does, and much of it she procures from her guests. The salmon came today from the gentleman over there with the white hair, for he owns a salmon river in Scotland. And the haunch of venison was sent by the man with the diamond-and-pearl stickpin in his cravat.''

"They know what she needs in advance, then?'' Rosalind seemed a little surprised.

"Of course. You see, she asks them for it, and they're glad enough to send it, for they nearly always taste it cooked better here than they've ever had it before. She has the finest chef and supervises her kitchens like a sergeant-major.'' Christopher grinned at the expression of amazement on her face.

After listening to several more of their hostess's blunt remarks, addressed to some of the most notable guests, Rosalind was forced to admit, "One cannot help but like her, you know. It's almost as though she's doing it deliberately, and with so many people of disparate interests and artistic talents someone such as her is needed to control them all. She was perfectly ready to listen to that poet for ten minutes, but then she made no bones about telling him that we had heard enough. And we had, of course.''

"I'm afraid that is typically her way of controlling the general conversation,'' Christopher explained to her, smiling a little ruefully. "I quickly found it prudent to do more listening than participating in the discussions, and now realize that I learn much more that way. Most evenings there is an intermingling of ministers, diplomats, scientists, poets, and artists, and I have come to realize and appreciate how skillful she is. Though inclined to be a trifle blunt at times, she also gives a good deal of encouragement when she deems it warranted.''

"Peter seems to be really enjoying himself at the moment,'' Judith remarked. "Who is that red-headed young lady he's sitting next to? I don't believe I've seen her at any of the balls or dinners we've attended.''

"She's more or less a poor relation of Lord Holland,'' Christopher said quietly, noting that Rosalind had also been watching her closely. "Her name is Miss Georgina Walters, and she has been staying here now for several weeks. You'll get a chance to meet her formally when the ladies retire and have tea. I believe she's somewhat timid, for she does not seem able to make friends easily, though the Hollands introduce her to a great many people, both ladies and gentlemen.''

Rosalind privately decided that Miss Walters would do better were she to listen more attentively to what her dinner partners had to say, instead of watching Christopher. The young lady had conversed with Peter, but other than that had scarcely taken her eyes from Christopher during the entire course of the meal.

She had to admit that Christopher was right in one respect, however, for when the ladies finally retired to the drawing room, leaving the gentlemen to their port and cigars, Miss Walters came over at once to where she and Judith were seated, and introduced herself.

"I've heard so much about you from Christopher," she said to Rosalind in sugary tones, "that I feel I already know you. He and I are, of course, the closest of friends."

Giving her a rather fixed smile, for she always disliked to be ignored, Judith asked, "Have you been in London long, Miss Walters? I do not recall having seen you at any of the balls and entertainments."

The other girl shook her head. "I'm afraid it is quite impossible for me to go out in the evenings, for Lady Holland makes it a practice to entertain dinner guests almost every night and, as so few ladies attend, I am needed to make the table a little less unequal."

Rosalind immediately felt sorry for her. Though she was thoroughly enjoying herself, it would be rather a strain to have to be present at a dinner of this sort every evening, with no one knowing just what Lady Holland might say next. She turned to Miss Walters with an expression of sympathy in her eyes. "I have found it one of the most diverting dinners I have ever attended," she said, "but I can readily apprehend how it must be to converse with people of such diverse opinions every single evening."

"Indeed it is," Miss Walters told her, "but Christopher is such a dear, understanding gentleman, and has made my many chores so much the lighter, that I don't know what I should do without him now.''

"Really?'' Rosalind said, her sympathy fast disappearing. "Do you act as Lady Holland's secretary, write invitations, letters and such for her?''

"Not as a rule, for she prefers to attend to her own correspondence,'' Miss Walters said, "but I try to be in the house in case she should need me for some chore or other. Christopher sometimes takes me for walks in Kensington Gardens just so that I can get out into a little fresh air. He says he likes to see the roses come to my cheeks.''

"Assisting Lady Holland must be an excellent training for when you marry,'' Rosalind said thoughtfully, "for I should think she is quite an organizer when it comes to dinners of this sort. The food tonight was some of the finest I can recall having eaten anywhere in London.''

"Lady Holland has a decided talent for political entertaining,'' Miss Walters agreed, though there was a coldness in her eyes as she looked at Rosalind, "and is training me so that I will make a good wife for a budding politician.''

It had sounded very much like a challenge, Rosalind thought, but one she meant to disregard completely, and when Judith started to ask the young woman questions about some of the other guests, she excused herself and went over to see how her mama was getting along with her hostess, for Lady Stockton did not look at all happy.

Lady Holland set no store by the usual way of having equal numbers of each sex at the table, and there was only one other female guest present that night, in addition to Lady Stockton and her daughters. Lady Parkinson, wife of Viscount Parkinson, was in complete agreement with her hostess on the need for women of a certain age to take to politics, influencing and leading their menfolk where possible, and she showed no hesitation in making her views known.

Lady Stockton, who was not at all averse to using her own persuasive powers upon her husband, was still quite shocked to hear the other two ladies speak as though it was their duty to bring their own influence to bear whenever possible, and most decidedly within their own households. During the course of the evening, however, she had heard sufficient of Lady Holland's tart tongue to persuade her to refrain from making her own feelings known. She could not recall when she had sat through such a dreadfully embarrassing dinner, though she, too, had to admit that the food was most decidedly superior to any offered elsewhere.

Her daughter's appearance at her side, though meant to comfort, only made her worry the more lest Rosalind say the wrong thing, and it was a profound relief to her when the gentlemen finally came into the drawing room. A half hour later they were able to leave without causing anay censorious comment from their hostess.

Once they were safely inside their own carriage, however, Lady Stockton could hold back her feelings no longer.

"I trust you found the evening as interesting as you expected to, my lord," she said to her husband, a tart note in her voice.

"As a matter of fact, I did, my dear. I cannot recall when I enjoyed a dinner party so much, for with a round table like that it was perfectly correct to speak to everyone present," he told her, deliberately ignoring her tones. "Peter seemed to be enjoying himself also, weren't you, my boy? And, as I've said before, that young man, Ferguson, is going to go a long way in the field of politics. He's got a sound head on his shoulders."

"I must agree, Papa," Peter put in. "He indubitably held his own with the gentlemen present this evening, and it was obvious that he was highly regarded. It was also quite evident that being a part of that household gives him an excellent opportunity for learning and advancement."

Lady Stockton sighed heavily. "I'm almost sorry that you two did not have to experience, after sitting through that woman's dictatorial handling of the entire dinner conversation, almost another hour of her and Lady Parkinson discussing how they could best influence, and even go so far as to lead, their husbands in matters of politics," Lady Stockton declared. "I have never in my entire life heard anything quite so ridiculous."

"Did you tell them how you felt in such a matter, my dear?" Lord Stockton asked, a hint of amusement in his voice.

"I most certainly did not," Lady Stockton said. "I, at least, behaved like a lady and allowed them to prattle on without making any comment myself."

Having consumed a considerable quantity of an excellent port, Lord Stockton was in no mood to quarrel with his wife. "Of course, my dear, you have never in your life attempted to influence me on any matters that were about to come before the House, have you?" he asked with a deep chuckle. "You haven't tried to persuade me that there should be a law to protect the young boys who climb up chimneys, and imprison the men who light fires under them to make them move faster?"

"Well, of course, I have discussed with you such inhuman treatment of those little boys," Lady Stockton said, sounding much aggrieved. "But I would never tell you how I think you should cast your vote. That is decidedly not the duty of a good wife and mother."

"I found their views most interesting, Mama," Rosalind said, "and I see no reason whatsoever why a wife should not explain to her husband how she feels about matters of considerable importance. After all, the laws which are being enacted will, in many instances, affect their children, and are of importance to the entire family."

Lady Stockton sighed heavily. "I knew that accepting their invitation was the wrong thing to do, but you would go there, my lord, and now you can see for yourself the results. As though Rosalind was not already quite unbiddable."

Unseen in the darkness of the carriage Rosalind's eyes flashed angrily. "I liked Lady Holland," she said, "and I thought that, though she was sometimes rude about it, and might have done so in a more polite way, she was behaving quite correctly in directing the dinner conversation. It is more than possible, of course, that her brusqueness is somewhat defensive, and may be brought about to some extent by the way some ladies cannot forget her past and refuse to join their husbands when invited to her home.''

"What did I tell you, my lord?" Lady Stockton asked in horror. "I knew that we ought not to have accepted, but you were the one who insisted, and now our daughter is speaking as though that woman's past had no significance whatsoever. And as for you, young lady, I should like to know from what source comes the information you have acquired about Lady Holland. If that young man to whom you seem to have taken a liking has been speaking to you of such things, then I do not wish to see him in my house again—''

"Now, my dear," Lord Stockton broke in, "don't you start jumping to conclusions. I don't think our daughter goes about with eyes and ears closed, and there are plenty of gossips in this town always ready to make mischief.''

"I have no intention of telling you where the information came from, Mama," Rosalind said sharply, "but even I would not think to discuss something of that sort with a gentleman. And I know that Mr. Ferguson would not ever think to malign his employer's wife.''

"What kind of gossip are you talking about?" Judith asked eagerly. "Surely you might have told me, for it would have made the evening decidedly more interesting. I, for one, was quite bored with all that talk of politics during dinner, and then, later, I was disappointed when not a single lady mentioned my pretty gown, or the unusual beading on my wrap. I've never worn them before without someone admiring them.''

"I know, my love," Lady Stockton said soothingly, "it was my fault for listening to your papa and taking you there, for it could not have been a very interesting evening for you.''

"At least Miss Walters was polite," Judith declared, "but when she began to speak of how friendly she is with Mr. Ferguson, Rosalind took offense, I believe, and decided not to listen to her anymore, but to join you, Mama.''

"And I dearly wished that she had not, for I then had the additional worry that my outspoken daughter might say the wrong thing," Lady Stockton said sharply, then as the carriage came to a halt she added, "I wish to speak with you before you retire for the evening, Rosalind. I'll come to your bed-chamber just as soon as Manners has put me into my dressing gown."

Lord Stockton, who was already out of the carriage and reaching up a hand to help his wife, protested mildly, "Don't you think it could wait until morning, my dear. It has been a rather tiring evening for all of us. You'll both feel much better at breakfast, I'm sure."

His wife was, however, adamant. "What I have to say is best said now, while it is on my mind, Geoffrey. I'll sleep much better for having said my piece."

As he reached up a hand to his older daughter, he shook his head slightly and Rosalind murmured, "Don't tease yourself, Papa. She'll be happier once it is off of her mind. And I'm really not too tired to listen."

He kissed her cheek. "I'll wish you a good night, then, my dear, and we'll talk about it over breakfast in the morning. I do believe that young Ferguson will be most successful in any venture he undertakes."

Rosalind followed Lady Stockton up the stairs, and was glad that Judith was so close behind them that her mama had no opportunity to make any further remarks about the evening. She had already said more than enough to make Judith ask a lot of awkward questions later.

Her gown was removed and put away, and she was already into her night rail when her mama came into the chamber. Hetty stayed long enough to help her young lady into a dressing gown, then hurried off.

"What is it, Mama?" Rosalind asked. "I am quite tired, and know that you must be also, so come quickly to the point, if you please."

"I shall come as quickly or as slowly as I choose, my girl, and you will have no say in the matter," Lady Stockton said, angry that her daughter had the audacity to give her orders. "I will say nothing for now about your conduct at the Hollands' dinner, but your remarks in the carriage were completely uncalled for, and I would like to know just how much you think you know about Lady Holland?''

Rosalind sighed. She was very tired, for her day had started with an early morning ride in the park with Peter, and it was now quite late.

"Even if I knew the reasons why Lady Holland is treated by some ladies of the *ton* as a social outcast, I would not repeat them to you or anyone else," she said quietly. "Nevertheless her reputation has been damaged, and that is what I referred to in the privacy of my family. If you are upset because I said that I liked her, I am sorry, but it happens to be true."

"I cannot think that any young lady who was in her right mind could possibly take a liking to such a dreadfully rude and out-spoken person," Lady Stockton emphatically declared, "and as for her reputation, I can assure you that it is most justly deserved, for—" She stopped as Rosalind put up a hand.

"I have no wish to know . . ." she began, but paused at the sound of another knock on her door, and Lord Stockton came in.

"Now, my dear," he said to his wife, taking her arm gently, "it is far too late for arguments, and I, for one, want to get some sleep. You have all day tomorrow to talk this thing out, if you still wish to, but I very much doubt you will be inclined to do so in the light of day. Try to get a good night's rest, Rosalind, and we'll see you in the morning."

He led Lady Stockton gently from the chamber, and closed the door quietly behind him.

A few minutes later, Rosalind got into bed and leaned over to put out the candle. She was extremely tired, but had serious doubts that she would be able to fall asleep right away, for the events of the evening seemed to be flitting around in her head.

Though she had taken little part in the conversations that went back and forth over the dinner table, she had found them to be extremely stimulating and they had opened her eyes to what at first seemed another world.

The events of the day had been discussed in depth, starting, of course, with Napoleon's escape and progress thus far through France, and here she had been rather shocked to find that Lady

Holland was a great admirer of the fallen emperor. She had, in fact, readily admitted that, with the consent of his jailers, she had supplied him with newspapers during his captivity on Elba.

Rosalind could not help wondering what it would be like to live in the kind of atmosphere that was present at Holland House that evening. For her it had not been dull for a single moment, whether they were discussing poetry, works of art, ratification of the Treaty of Peace with America, or the recent riots that had taken place—those in London against enactment of the Corn Bill, and in the north of England for higher wages in the colliery trade.

Rosalind had not at first cared much for Miss Walters, but when they retired to the drawing room she had seemed all that was amiable until she tried to indicate that she was on close terms with Christopher Ferguson, and this Rosalind simply could not, and would not, believe.

Chapter Eight

The following morning Lady Stockton slept late and had breakfast in bed, but when she finally came down the stairs and went into the room at the back of the house where she kept her household accounts and such, she inquired if her older daughter was still indoors. When the reply was in the affirmative, she sent for her at once.

A few minutes later there was a knock on the door, and Rosalind entered.

"Good morning, Mama," she said, then crossed the room and gave Lady Stockton a warm hug and a kiss on her cheek. "I trust you slept well last night."

"As a matter of fact, I did not, and I am sorry to say that you have a good deal to do with it," Lady Stockton snapped. "I can blame no one but myself for accepting that invitation, but I must tell you that I was completely disconcerted to find that you did not share my feelings of revulsion for that dreadful woman."

Realizing that the meeting was bound to be somewhat lengthy, Rosalind drew up a chair for herself, and sat facing her mama across the small desk. There was no question but that Lady Stockton looked as though she had slept badly last night, for her complexion was paler than usual and there were dark rings under her eyes.

"It would seem that you are quite infatuated with Mr. Ferguson, and though your papa does not share my views, I must still tell you that I only wish it had been his brother you had formed an attachment to," Lady Stockton said with a sigh. "As your mama, what I would now like to know is where and when you first met Mr. Ferguson, and what exactly happened on that occasion."

Though Rosalind merely shrugged slightly, her cheeks gave her away, for they turned a quite noticeable shade of pink.

"It was the day of the christening at Belvoir Castle," she said quietly. "When Judith and I left you to take a tour of the newly renovated rooms, she quite naturally wished to join friends of her own age, so I saw her safely into the hands of Lady Goodwin and her daughter. After I had seen as much of the rooms as I wished—it was very warm and dreadfully noisy, if you recall—I decided to take a stroll into the main conservatory to see what trees and plants were in bloom."

Lady Stockton's eyebrows rose, but she made no comment.

"The gardeners, who know me very well, must have been celebrating in the kitchen," Rosalind went on, "for it was quite empty, and blessedly peaceful, so I sat down on a bench for a while, and it was then that Mr. Ferguson appeared and asked if he might join me."

"And that was all? Do you expect me to believe that he just sat there in silence?" Lady Stockton demanded.

"We did nothing amiss," Rosalind said. "We talked about all manner of things, then suddenly the gardeners' voices could be heard from the far end of the conservatory, and I got up and hurried away before they saw me."

"And you never made any attempt to get in touch with each other after that?" asked Lady Stockton, an expression of complete disbelief on her face.

Rosalind gave her a strange smile. "We quite forgot to exchange names," she said simply. "Though I did not know it at the time, he had apparently been wounded and was on sick leave, helping Lord Holland, and shortly after that he returned to the wars."

Lady Stockton looked at her daughter's face, at the steady blue eyes, at the generous mouth, and at the firm set of her jaws, and knew that she had little chance of persuading her to comply with her next request.

"I do not want you to mingle with people like Lady Holland," she said quietly. "I was shocked that you could have taken a liking to a woman of that sort, and I do not wish for a daughter of mine to adopt her ways. I would prefer that you do not see Mr. Ferguson again."

"Does Papa feel as you do?" Rosalind asked in a shocked voice.

"Not at the moment, but I am sure I can persuade him to my way of thinking if it should come to that," Lady Stockton said, more confidently than she felt. "I mean to make it clear to Mr. Ferguson that we will never permit him to marry you."

Rosalind looked at her mama, who had been allowed to marry the man she loved, and who had every bit as much of a say as to what went on in her own house as did Lady Holland, but in a much more subtle way. "What would you have done had your parents forbade you to see Papa?" she asked.

"My parents completely approved of your papa," Lady Stockton said self-righteously.

"That was not what I asked. What would you have done if they had not approved of him and had forbade you to see him?" Rosalind repeated.

"I should have done as they wished, of course," Lady Stockton said, quite decidedly, "for I knew for a certainty that they wanted only what was best for me, as your papa and I do for you."

"Then I congratulate you, for you were more fortunate than I in your choice of parents," Rosalind said dryly. "I will not give Christopher up after finding him again."

Without waiting for a response from her mama, she turned and walked out of the room, then hurried upstairs to don her pelisse. Fortunately, Hetty was in the bedchamber putting away some gowns, and she ran down the backstairs at once to fetch her cape and accompany her young mistress.

They walked for miles without a single word having passed between them, and afterward Rosalind could not have told anyone where she had been. Eventually she realized that the sun was sinking, and that Hetty must be feeling tired, hungry, and footsore. Seeing a cab rank, she hired a hansom and had it take them back to Upper Brook Street.

"You hurry inside, Hetty," she said, "while I pay the cabbie."

But before she had taken the money from her purse, her papa was there, paying off the man then placing an arm around her shoulders and drawing her inside the house and toward his study.

"Where have you been, my dear?" he asked, not unkindly. "We've been most concerned about you all day."

"I really don't know," she told him, realizing that she had not the slightest idea. "I needed to think, so we just walked on and on, until I suddenly realized the sun was going down and Hetty was limping, so I got a hackney and came home."

"And did you solve anything?" he asked.

She shook her head. "No, but I won't give him up unless he doesn't want me. I don't care what Mama says."

He raised his eyebrows. "Is that what it was all about?" he asked.

She nodded. "She said that I am not to see him again."

He sighed and shook his head. "Don't worry about it anymore. I'll take care of it. Run upstairs now and rest for a while before dinner. You look worn out, my dear," he told her, smiling benignly.

She slept, and dreamed of Christopher, then awoke to find herself alone, quite chilly as the fire had burned low, and with only fifteen minutes left before the dinner hour.

There was a knock on the door, and Hetty hurried in. Rosalind watched her take out the gown she had already planned to wear, then allowed the girl to dress her and make her hair look a little more tidy. Then she went down the stairs and met the rest of the family as they were just going toward the dining room.

Lord Stockton put an arm around her shoulders. "Are you feeling better now, my dear?" he asked.

"Yes. I fell into a deep sleep," she told him, "and I do not believe I'm fully awake even now."

He chuckled. "You're not, but by the time you get some food into you, everything will seem much better."

As usual, he was right, it did seem better, mostly because her mama appeared to be no longer at odds with her, and even spoke of their plans for attending Almack's the following evening, just as if nothing had passed between them that morning.

Lady Stockton did not, in fact, mention the subject to Rosalind again, and appeared not to mind in the least when Christopher Ferguson danced both waltzes with Rosalind, and took her to partake of the light refreshments that passed for supper at Almack's.

No doubt the fact that Lord Graystone danced with Judith and escorted her into supper had something to do with this, for, to Rosalind's profound relief, Lady Stockton beamed as her friends eyed her jealously and commented on the good looks and charming manners of the two brothers.

But, excepting when they were dancing, when other couples were always close by, there was no time that evening for Rosalind to speak to Christopher alone. After the first waltz she began to steer him toward the potted palms, but her mama seemed to step out of nowhere, to engage Christopher in a conversation so trivial and foolish that it was obvious she was saying the first thing that came into her head. And all Rosalind's pointed stares could not budge her until the music started for the next dance.

It was Judith who ruined the next opportunity, for as the music stopped, she was beside Rosalind, begging her to help her fix a torn hem, and Christopher could only smile somewhat ruefully and permit Judith to drag her away to the ladies' retiring room.

Surprisingly, Judith's manners showed a most decided improvement as she saw more and more of Lord Graystone, and she and Rosalind got along together much better than they had ever done in the past.

But for the present neither gentleman seemed at all desirous of making any commitment. It was not known when Christopher, and many of the other gentlemen they danced with nightly, would be leaving for Brussels, for Napoleon's progress had slowed as he proceeded north, through France. He was, quite obviously, not anxious to go to war again until he had the number of men he wanted behind him.

Lord Graystone's father had persuaded him that he should not risk his life again, as he was his only son, and so Christopher would go alone when the time came, which was now thought to be in late May or even June.

Tomorrow night was Judith's come-out ball, which probably accounted, in part, for Lady Stockton's sudden lack of interest in Rosalind's beau, for she had been busy for days with preparations for the big event.

The next morning the entire house was at sixes and sevens. Footmen hurried about taking chairs and tables out of rooms, and putting others in their place. Arms full of flowers and a great many potted plants were delivered, and when Rosalind went to the kitchen with a message, she declared that she had never seen it so busy, or smelled so many tantalizing odors as their chef worked with the caterers on the evening's fare. She was forced to admit, however, that on the day of her own come-out she had not been allowed to go near the kitchen.

As she came back into the hall she was just in time to catch her mama as she hurried from the drawing room, and to take another half dozen or so tasks off her busy hands.

"And you might run upstairs and see how Judith is going along," Lady Stockton added. "I told her she was to rest this morning, and then, after a light luncheon, she might come down and take a look at the ballroom, but under no circumstances was she to worry about anything not yet accomplished."

Rosalind grinned. "I know the rest," she said, "for I clearly recall when I had that privilege. After viewing the frantic activity in the ballroom, I was to take a leisurely bath and dream of all the beaus I would enchant that evening. My hair was washed and dried and brushed until it shone, and Hetty stayed with me, at my beck and call all day long, applying creams to my hands and arms to make them soft and white, filing my nails and buffing them to a pretty sheen, and polishing my newly washed hair until it also gleamed.''

She did not have the heart to tell her mama that she had grown so bored that she had sent Hetty for two packs of cards. She had then spent a couple of hours teaching the girl to play piquet, an arduous and absorbing task that effectively took away the butterflies that had, up to that point, persisted in fluttering around inside of her. She somehow doubted that Judith felt as nervous as she had, but she had meant to go up to her chamber even before her mama had suggested it, just to make sure.

''Oh, you must look at the card Lord Graystone sent with his posy, Rosalind. It is, of course, the one I shall carry tonight,'' Judith declared, the minute her sister stepped inside the door. ''He has written, in his own hand, I am sure, 'To Judith, flower of youth and beauty's pride.' Doesn't he have a way with words?''

Rosalind smiled and said, ''He most certainly does,'' for she would not have thought, for a moment, of telling her the quotation was Dryden's. ''How do you feel? Not even a little nervous about this evening?''

''Oh, no,'' Judith said assuredly, ''I mean to enjoy myself enormously, for my come-out party is bound to be the very finest of the Season. Mama keeps coming in to tell me how everything is going along, and though I know she must be quite frantic, today she doesn't dare tell me any of the problems.''

''Just make the most of it,'' Rosalind warned her, ''for I know from experience that this is the only time you will ever receive such preferential treatment.''

''I'm sure I will on my wedding day,'' Judith said slyly. ''You haven't experienced that as yet, but I do recall that when Patricia got married we weren't allowed to say anything that might upset her.''

''And you did, if I remember correctly,'' Rosalind said, her eyes twinkling, ''and only the fact that you were a bridesmaid prevented Mama from confining you to your chamber for the rest of the day.''

Judith chuckled gleefully. "All I did was tell her that her bouquet had been dropped in the mud and all the flower stems smashed," she said, adding, "and she believed me, of course."

"Well," Rosalind told her, "while you ponder your past misdeeds, I'll run along and see what else I can do to help. Every time I see Mama she gives me another dozen or so chores, and I'm beginning to wonder where she's getting them all from. I'll come back and see you when the hairdresser arrives, for they always want to cut too much off, and you'll need help in stopping her."

She hurried out, and went in search of her mama, for despite her words, she was a little worried that Lady Stockton was doing too much, and would be exhausted before the first guest arrived.

In the end, Rosalind had to enlist her papa's aid, for Lady Stockton was sure that nothing would be done correctly unless she did it herself, and only Lord Stockton's firm hand on her arm escorting her up the stairs and to her chamber, ensured that she took a much-needed couple of hours' rest after luncheon.

Lord Graystone and Mr. Ferguson had been invited to the private dinner that preceded the ball, along with the Clearys and a number of close friends and relatives of the Stocktons. Most of them were already gathered in the drawing room when Rosalind came down the stairs, and she stood in the doorway for a moment, secretly counting heads to see if everyone had arrived.

"Is anyone missing?" Christopher asked, with a twinkle in his eyes.

He was surprised when she turned a serious face to his and said, "Not really. Everyone is here except for Aunt Genevieve and Uncle Herbert, I believe, and I heard them in the hall just a moment ago. Judith means to make an entrance, you see, and she says she'll not come down until everyone is present."

"I was joking," he told her, grinning and shaking his head. "I'd no idea that you were actually counting. The little minx means to have her way this evening if no other time, I suppose.

Did you behave in that way when you had your come-out?''

Rosalind shook her head. ''I was terribly nervous, for my ball was one of the first of the Season, and I really did not yet know many young people. But I must say that once it was over I seemed to have a host of friends wherever I went.''

Just then the butler announced Lord and Lady Greenhough, and she murmured, ''Please excuse me, for I must greet them and then let Judith know she can come down at last.''

His eyes followed her as she seemed almost to float toward the door, a vision in amber-colored lace several shades paler than her glorious chestnut hair. Tonight her hair was most becomingly piled high on top of her head, with just a few curls straggling artfully around her ears and onto her creamy shoulders.

She curtsied to the couple, welcoming them warmly, then excused herself. ''I really must make sure everything is all right with my sister,'' she said, then hurried toward the curved staircase.

Hetty was waiting just around the curve, hidden from sight, and at Rosalind's slight nod she gave a signal to Judith and the latter came out of her bedchamber and met her sister at the top of the stairs.

Gowned in the traditional white, at first glance she looked demure until one noticed the tilt of her chin, and a firmness in the way she held her head. In one gloved hand she carried a posy of deep pink roses and lilies of the valley, which had, of course, been sent by Lord Graystone. She was already enjoying herself immensely, and as she slipped her other hand into Rosalind's, she gave it a meaningful squeeze.

''If I don't get a chance to say so later, Ros,'' she said quietly, ''I must tell you how much I appreciate all you've done for me. I mean to have a wonderful Season and, at the end of it, marry very well indeed.''

Rosalind chuckled. ''I believe you will at that,'' she replied. ''Just remember, though, you must allow the lucky gentleman to think that he is doing the chasing.''

They started down the stairs as the guests came out of the

drawing room to watch them, and the murmur of approval could be clearly heard.

Everyone gathered around the two girls, murmuring compliments, and then Lady Stockton unobtrusively guided the gentlemen to their dinner partners and the party went into the dining room.

Earlier in the day, Rosalind had checked the seating arrangements and made sure that she was placed next to Christopher, and it seemed for today at least, that her mama had called a halt to her attempts to put an end to their relationship.

"You missed your drink before dinner," he told her as he seated her beside him, "but I believe it was worth it, for the two of you looked very lovely as you came down the stairs. Whoever chose that color for you had excellent taste."

"Thank you for the compliment, sir," Rosalind murmured, her eyes twinkling, "for it was I who chose it."

"And thank you for carrying my flowers," he said, motioning toward the posys of forget-me-nots and yellow rosebuds, which she had placed on the table. "I'm sure that both of you must have received a great many flowers from admirers today."

Rosalind nodded, for there was no point in telling him otherwise. "Judith's bedchamber was much like a conservatory, and I did have a few bouquets myself," she admitted. "It's all part of the pleasure and gaiety of the occasion. And why not, for a girl only has one night quite like this in her whole lifetime."

"For which her parents must be vastly relieved, for I should imagine the cost to be most excessive, and put a tremendous burden on parents with many daughters," he said thoughtfully.

Rosalind nodded. "It is made even worse, of course, because at this time of year all the merchants take advantage and double their prices for everything, including almost every part of the meal such as this. You simply wouldn't believe what we had to pay for green peas."

"I most certainly would," he said with mock gravity, "for I handle much of the Hollands' living expenses in addition to the political work."

She smiled a little sadly. There were so many things she

wanted to ask him about himself, but could not do so when they were with the others. And though her mama had not once referred to that dreadful conversation on the morning after the dinner at the Hollands, it seemed as though she was quite deliberately preventing them from ever being alone, as if she knew that more had occurred at their first meeting than just conversation. But she would be very busy with Judith this evening, and perhaps, Rosalind thought, if they were very, very careful, she and Christopher might be able to slip out into the garden unobserved.

Under the table his leg was pressing against hers, and she wondered if he was as aware of it as she was, but when it moved away and then came back, she knew for sure that it was quite deliberate, and the knowledge made it more than a little exciting.

"Is your program completely filled?" he asked softly.

"Why, sir, what a question to ask a lady when you have already reserved your dances," she said lightly, not sure why he was asking.

"I just wondered if you might need a little air at some time during the evening. If the gentleman whose dance it was began searching for you, it could be embarrassing," he murmured.

"But I suppose I could," she began, speaking normally at first, then lowering her voice, "write in the name of someone who would never ask me . . ." she whispered, not daring to look at him, but concentrating, instead, on pushing a piece of fish around her plate.

"You are most perceptive, Miss Marshall," he said aloud, then added softly, "Just let me know which one."

A glance around reassured Rosalind that no one, not even her mama, was looking at all suspiciously their way. "I believe you requested the dance before supper with me, did you not?" she asked him, "but I'm not sure if you wrote it down. Just let me take a look."

As she opened her evening reticule she smiled at Lord Horton, the gentleman on her left, then handed her program to Christopher.

"You're quite right," he said, taking a pencil and writing

on the card. "There, how remiss of me. I would have been devastated if someone else had come along and stolen you from under my nose."

"Don't put that away if you have any dances left," Lord Horton requested, "for I would hate to miss this opportunity and find that there were none left later."

He was the old friend of Peter's who had been with him the night they had spent at the inn, and who had met her the next morning as she went to make sure that her brother was awake. She now knew him very well and liked him tremendously as a friend, and she gladly allowed him to put his name down. He was by no means a fool, however, and she could not help but wonder if he had heard any part of her conversation with Christopher. The expression in his eyes as he returned the card told her that he had, but, fortunately, he would be just about the last person to tell her mama.

Once the lengthy meal was at an end, guests seemed to pour into the house, until Rosalind began to wonder if her mama had, perhaps, sent out too many invitations. She knew, however, that only if it were said to be a most frightful crush would the party be deemed truly successful.

Excusing herself from her dinner partners, she made her way to the ballroom to watch her papa lead Judith into the first dance, then Peter and her mama joined them, and only when the two couples had changed partners with each other, did the other guests join in.

After that the evening seemed to fly, and before she knew it Christopher was at her side, leading her out for the waltz before supper. Though it was crowded, and they could not move as quickly around the floor as she liked, it was wonderful to be in his arms again, and her only regret was that it ended much too soon.

The family were together for supper, though Lady Stockton spent little time at the table for she simply could not forgo greeting each and every one of her old friends and receiving their congratulations on her triumph, for this was indeed the party of the year thus far.

"I can see you're not enjoying yourself one bit." Rosalind teased her sister as she passed behind her chair, and was delighted to catch a glimpse of a most tender look on Lord Graystone's face as he gazed at Judith.

How wonderful it would be, she thought, if the two of them were to make a match of it, for Timothy Graystone was one of the nicest men she had ever met, and she would be delighted to have him as a brother-in-law. Surely their mama would be satisfied if that should happen, and leave her to the brother of her choice.

When they went back into the ballroom after supper, Rosalind could hardly bear to wait three more dances before she could disappear into the garden and meet Christopher. What if her mama, who had been happily visiting with one and then another of her friends, should decide to watch the dancers for the fourth dance, and find that she was not one of them?

Somehow she smiled and chattered to her partners, and her feet, completely accustomed to the various movements, took her through each figure of all three dances, but she could not have told anyone afterward what the dances were and who her partners had been. And then the musicians began to tune their instruments and the gentlemen sought their partners for the fourth dance after supper.

She caught a glimpse of her mama, standing with her back to the floor talking to a friend at the opposite side of the ballroom, before she quickly slipped through the French doors and hurried to where she could barely make out Christopher standing near a small tree.

Just before she got there, however, the toe of her slipper caught in a crack in the footpath, and she fell into his arms in a way that she had definitely not intended. He held her close for several wonderful minutes, and she could feel his heart beating and smell a heady masculine scent of tobacco, pomade, and port, and then she regained her breath, and he released her but retained a hold on one gloved hand.

"Are you all right now?" he asked, with a touch of amusement in his voice. "I'm not quite used to young ladies throwing themselves into my arms, you know."

"Yes, I'm quite all right," she said, laughing now that the certain fall had been avoided. "I'd forgotten that the path here is broken in parts, but it feels so good to see you alone at last."

"I must admit that I'm a little confused," he told her. "Lord Stockton appears to completely approve of me, but your mama seems to be determined to make sure that we're never alone, even in an open carriage. Surely she must realize by now that I am not about to do you harm?"

"It's Lady Holland she has taken in dislike," Rosalind tried to explain, "and she is convinced that I will become exactly like her if I continue to see you."

"There's no danger of that, my dear," he told her, "for though I have become very fond of Lady Holland, I would never permit a wife of mine to behave in the way that she does. It suits Lord Holland admirably, but I'm afraid that it would not suit me at all."

There was a gasp from Rosalind, but before she could say a word, Christopher continued.

"This is not a proposal of marriage," he said quietly, "for I do not consider myself to be, as yet, in a position to take a wife, no matter how much I might feel about a certain young lady. Also, I cannot guarantee that, when we face Napoleon for the last time, I will come home in one piece."

"Must you go?" she asked, in a voice choked with tears.

"Yes, I must," he told her, "for at the moment it's the only way I can serve my country. If all goes well there, I hope to be able to serve her at home just as loyally, but in a more peaceful fashion."

He stroked her cheek with the tip of his finger.

"I love you more than I can say, more than I ever thought possible, but I cannot ask you to wait for me, for that would not be fair," he said quietly. "And I cannot even promise that when I return I will be in a position to marry you and keep you in the way to which you are accustomed, for though I am by no means starving, I do not have either the money or the title my brother can offer."

"Your brother is falling in love with Judith," Rosalind told him quietly.

"Is he, by Jove?" Christopher said. "I must not have been watching them very carefully."

Just then the figure of Lady Stockton could be seen looking out through the French doors, and then she started slowly toward them.

A familiar voice behind them said, very quietly, "I have been with you all the time. Don't forget. We both brought Rosalind out for some fresh air."

"Robert," Rosalind gasped, but there was no time to say anything else for Lady Stockton had seen them and was hurrying forward.

"Lady Stockton," Lord Horton said, with a slight bow, "isn't it delightful out here this evening? Rosalind was feeling slightly overheated and so we brought her out here for a breath of air."

With an almost audible sigh of relief, Lady Stockton turned to her daughter. "Are you all right now, my dear? I really don't blame you, for it has become very warm inside, and I expect quite a few people will come out when this dance finishes. Perhaps I should have some more lanterns brought out."

"Don't you do it, Mama. I'll go and tell Walters to take care of it, if you like," Rosalind put in quickly.

"Thank you, my love," Lady Stockton murmured, smiling vaguely at the two gentlemen as she started for the door with her daughter. "Tell him that three or four additional ones will be enough."

As soon as they were alone, Christopher turned to the other man. "Though I appreciate your intervention for Rosalind's sake, sir, I cannot help but think that you were deliberately eavesdropping on a private conversation."

"Not deliberately, sir," Lord Horton told him. "I came out first, knowing, I must admit, that you two had planned a rendezvous, but I'm afraid I thought it would be something it was most decidedly not."

"You thought I meant to harm her?" Christopher was almost choking with anger.

"I did not know you at all, sir, so how could I tell? You must know that Rosalind is of a rather impetuous nature and I wished to make sure, on behalf of her family, that she came to no harm." Lord Horton's voice sounded as reasonable as his words. "When I found that you were a man of unusual honor, I did not make my presence known, and my only regret was that I could not depart without being seen by one or other of you. I am glad that by my presence here I was able to be of service, and assure you that nothing I heard will go any further."

"I don't believe we have met, sir," Christopher said, holding out his hand. "I am Christopher Ferguson."

Horton took it in a firm clasp. "Robert Horton, sir, at your service, and I give you my best wishes for success in all your ventures, particularly the battle with Napoleon," he said. "I'm a good friend of Rosalind's brother, Peter, but I've known Rosalind only this Season, as I, too, was on the Peninsula, helping to defeat Napoleon. She's somewhat unusual for a young lady, but game as can be, and I wish you both every happiness. Perhaps we will meet again in Brussels very shortly."

They moved indoors together, then went their separate ways, each feeling a good deal better for having made the other's acquaintance.

Chapter Nine

The Stockton household slept late on the morning following the ball, which was, of course, completely understandable, and once they awoke they all called for breakfast to be served in their bedchambers.

In the master suite there was considerable discussion between Lord Stockton and his lady, and the topic was, once again, their older daughter's relationship with Mr. Ferguson.

"I tell you, Geoffrey," Lady Stockton said, "Rosalind is completely infatuated with that young man, and from what I can see—living with and working for the Hollands as he does—he probably has no means of supporting himself let alone a wife and children. Surely he would have rooms of his own elsewhere if he could afford them? What will you do if they suddenly run off together?"

"I'm convinced that he is far too honorable to do anything of that sort," her husband assured her. "Mind you, I'd not put Rosalind past trying to talk him into it. But he's determined to help put down Napoleon once and for all, and until he's seen that through I'm sure he will not even consider marriage. I've taken a liking to him, my love, and only wish a way could be seen for them to make a match of it."

"Please don't think that I dislike him, Geoffrey," Lady Stockton said. "He is most personable, dresses quite conservatively, and seems to be extremely sensible, but I still have a dreadful feeling that he had enticed Rosalind into the garden last evening, and that Robert Horton had come to her rescue.''

"Knowing our daughter, it's more likely that she did the enticing," he said with a grunt. "Did she look at all flustered, her hair disturbed, her cheeks flushed, or any of the ways young ladies are supposed to appear when they have just been kissed?''

"No, she didn't, and as a matter of fact I was surprised when I saw her more clearly, just inside the ballroom, for there was not even a hair out of place. But what would you know about the way young ladies look at such times, sir? You certainly never kissed me before we were married," she declared accusingly.

"Didn't I?" he asked, chuckling. "Well, perhaps you're right and it was someone else I was thinking of. Maybe one of the Peterson sisters, or Miss Pringle, the vicar's daughter. They were all a bit partial to me, if I recall.''

"Oh, you, with your teasing," she said, dimpling and blushing like a young girl. "I know quite well that you never had anything to do with any young lady once you met me. Stop trying to make me cross.''

"Not once I met you, my love, but I had quite a number of years before that to sow a few wild oats, you know." There was a twinkle in his eyes, giving away the fact that he was still trying to get her dander up.

"Now, just you be careful what you say," she told him, pretending to be angry but unable to keep her face straight, "and let us get back to the problem of our girls. I don't know why they couldn't behave as Patricia did. She was a pattern card of how a young girl should perform in her first Season. You'll have to have a word with that young man, that's all, and tell him he must leave her alone.''

"He's not offered for her as yet, my love, and as I said, he's not likely to until this thing in Brussels is taken care of. I can hardly suggest that he's unsuitable without saying what he's unsuitable for," Lord Stockton argued. "And does it occur to you that if we make it clear that Ferguson is not welcome here, it is quite possible that Lord Graystone will stay away also?''

Lady Stockton looked aghast. ''You surely don't think he would do that, Geoffrey? Judith would be heartbroken if he did, for you remember I am sure how she was almost walking on air last night before she went to bed.''

''It's bound to cause some repercussions, my dear,'' he said firmly. ''Why not let me just have a talk with Ferguson without laying down any rules but appealing to his own conscience, for I'm sure he has one. I might be able to ask him just to stay away for a while and see how they both go along after that.''

She sighed. ''Do what you think best, dear, for I am only trying to secure my daughter's happiness. If he stays away and Rosalind's infatuation does not fade, then we'll have to think further about it, that's all.''

''If it didn't fade in more than a year, it's not very likely to do so now when they're both in town and bound to see each other elsewhere, even if he doesn't call here,'' Lord Stockton said sensibly.

''But we have to try something,'' Lady Stockton told him, ''or else we'll end up with a daughter exactly like that horrid woman, and we'd be ashamed to even have her visit us in our home.''

Though Lord Stockton knew that his wife was grossly exaggerating Lady Holland's faults, he was becoming somewhat tired of arguing with her, and finally agreed to at least have a word with Ferguson. He could, after all, put it to him man to man and see how the fellow felt. He might even volunteer to stay away for a while to let her have a chance to meet someone else.

The opportunity came that afternoon when the two brothers paid a call, supposedly to find out how the family felt after their outstanding achievement of the night before. They reported that everyone they met as they drove through the park was talking of nothing else.

Lady Stockton almost preened as they told her what first one and then another had said, but then she remembered that this was the opportunity her husband needed and she gave him a meaningful glance.

He cleared his throat. "I'm glad you called today, Mr. Ferguson," he began, "for I received some information on a bill that is about to be presented, and wondered if you could spare the time to step into my study and clear up some questions I have on the Whig point of view."

Christopher smiled. "I'd be glad to, sir," he said. "Is it convenient to do so right now?"

"Fine," Lord Stockton said with a nod, and started toward the door with Christopher close behind him.

The young man could not fail to notice Rosalind's decidedly suspicious expression, but he gave her a reassuring smile and continued to follow her father out of the drawing room and into the study.

Closing the door behind him, Lord Stockton indicated a chair by the fireplace instead of in front of the desk, for he wanted this talk to be as informal as was possible under the circumstances. He took a chair across from the young man.

"There is no bill," Lord Stockton said abruptly, looking directly at his guest. "I had to use some excuse to stop my daughter becoming suspicious, for she's more than capable of insisting on joining us, and I wanted to have a quiet talk with you alone."

"I rather thought that was the case, sir," Ferguson said quite equably. "What can I do for you?"

"I very much enjoyed dinner at Holland House, and really appreciated the invitation, but I'm afraid that Lady Stockton did not share my feelings," he began. "In fact, she took Lady Holland in the greatest aversion, and has formed the opinion that Rosalind might quite easily become like that lady if she were in a position to see much of her."

It was quite obvious that Lord Stockton was finding it difficult to express himself, and, after waiting a moment, Ferguson said, "Lady Holland is actually a wonderful woman, sir, but there are a great many ladies of the *ton* who felt as Lady Stockton did on first meeting her, but changed their minds when they came to know her better.''

"My wife does not intend to try to improve on the acquaintanceship,'' Lord Stockton said dryly, and Ferguson smiled a little grimly.

''The thing is,'' Stockton continued, ''she is concerned as to where a relationship with you might lead our daughter. You see, we found it convenient for Rosalind to be taught by Peter's tutor, and as a consequence she received a much more extensive education than either of our other daughters. The result is, I regret to say, that she has become far too interested in politics for a young lady, which is why she was probably drawn to you in the first place.''

Ferguson shook his head. "Neither of us knew who the other was when we first met,'' he said quietly, ''and politics was decidedly not a topic of discussion on that occasion.''

Lord Stockton remembered what his wife had told him of that meeting, and he flushed a little and murmured, ''Mm, just so,'' for, unlike Lady Stockton, he had no wish to pry into what they might have spoken of instead.

''The thing is,'' he began again, ''Lady Stockton does not want Rosalind to become at all like Lady Holland.''

''I can assure you that there is no danger of that, sir, for their personalities are completely different, though they might become friends, which I am sure Lady Stockton would not at all care for. Is that not so?''

''Exactly, my boy. Knew you'd get my meaning,'' Stockton told him appreciatively.

''You misapprehend, sir,'' Ferguson said gently. ''I really have no idea what you or Lady Stockton want from me. I am not, at the moment, in a position to propose marriage to Rosalind, if that is what worries you, and I will not be until this thing with Napoleon is finished and done with.''

''No! Precisely!'' Lord Stockton said sharply. ''Thing is, my boy, it don't look to us as though you'll ever be in such a position, you not even living in a lodging of your own, but staying with the Hollands instead.''

"Appearances sometimes tend to be deceptive," Ferguson remarked mildly. "Don't you agree?"

Lord Stockton nodded. "Can be deceptive, of course, but what are people to think?"

"Frankly, I have been agreeably surprised that since my brother insisted I go about in London society, no one has questioned my right to do so—until now," Ferguson offered, his eyebrows raised slightly.

"I'm not questioning it either," Lord Stockton hastened to tell him. "Don't mistake me, my boy, it's just that my daughter has a fairly substantial dowry, and I'd not want to see her marry a pauper."

Ferguson smiled a little grimly. "You mean then, that before I even ask for her hand—which I am not in a position to do at the moment—you are asking me about my financial prospects?" he asked.

Lord Stockton looked apologetic. "It does sound to be not quite the thing, I know," he said quietly, "but I'm sure you've no prospects forthcoming from the Earl of Glastonbury, as he is not your own father. We really don't want our daughter to keep on seeing you, only to find that you have no means of supporting her if you do decide you wish to wed her."

"I can see your point, sir," Ferguson said, almost a little too mildly, "and there is no doubt whatsoever that Rosalind could easily find someone with much better financial prospects than I, but I do not think she would find anyone more capable of making her happy. Is there someone else, at the moment, from whom you feel you might receive an offer?"

"Not to my knowledge, although young Cleary had been seeing quite a lot of her until you came onto the scene. If you will agree not to see Rosalind for the time being, I will give you my word that I'll let you know in advance should a betrothal seem pending." Lord Stockton told him, "But I should think that your best bet would be to find yourself a wealthy widow, young man. There are a few of them about, you know."

"None that can compare to Rosalind, sir," Ferguson said, rising. "I will take your suggestion under advisement, and if it is your wish that I desist from paying calls upon your daughter, then I have no alternative but to comply. I cannot blame you, or your wife, for trying to protect her, but neither of you need have worried, for one moment, that I would ever do her harm.''

Lord Stockton sat in his study for a long time after Ferguson had left, feeling that he had handled the matter very badly, but not sure just where he had gone wrong. He was no wiser now about the fellow's financial position than he had been when Ferguson first entered the room, and he had a feeling that Ferguson was nowhere near as poor as Lady Stockton seemed to think. One thing had happened, however, and that was that the young man had risen even further in his estimation than before. He felt sure he would make a fine politician, and a fine husband for Rosalind, if he should ever get the chance.

When Christopher left Lord Stockton's study, he returned to the drawing room where his brother was waiting to leave, for he had already stayed longer than usual for an afternoon call. Rosalind looked most disappointed for she had hardly had the opportunity to say a word to Christopher.

They said their goodbyes to the young ladies, promising to see them later at Lady Charlesworth's musical evening, then, when they were settled in the carriage on their way to Holland House, Timothy asked his brother what Lord Stockton had wanted, for the request to speak to him had sounded most peculiar even to his ears.

''But that's outrageous,'' Timothy said when Christopher had outlined briefly what had passed between him and Lord Stockton. ''It's one thing inquiring about a gentleman's financial prospects if he is asking for a daughter's hand, but quite another matter when he hasn't yet proposed. You do want her, though, don't you?''

Christopher smiled. ''Oh, yes, I do most definitely want her, but I don't want to make any commitments until this business of Napoleon is out of the way for good.'' He chuckled. ''I'm sure Lord Stockton would not have said a word had it not been for his lady badgering him. She apparently took a dislike to Lady Holland as I had, frankly, expected her to.''

"I really cannot blame her for that," Timothy said with a wry smile. "That lady is a little difficult to take except in the smallest of doses. However, I think that you have little cause for worry. Rosalind loves you, and will most definitely wait for you until the time is right, and when the Stocktons find out that you are well enough placed, they'll drop all objections."

"He's indicated that he would prefer that I not call upon her for the time being," Christopher said. "If you get the opportunity before I do, I wish you would explain to her that my absence is not by any choice of mine."

"You'd best tell her yourself tonight," Timothy said firmly, "for I will certainly not visit a house where my own brother is not welcome."

"Come now, Timothy, you don't have to do that. I thought you were becoming somewhat interested in the young one and, if so, you certainly won't want to stay away," Christopher said.

But his brother was adamant. "You should not have to do so," he said, "and I feel I must indicate my displeasure at their attitude."

Christopher shrugged. When his younger brother came to a decision it was always difficult to budge him, and even more so when family pride was at stake.

They went together to the musical evening, as they often did, for Christopher had not gone to the trouble, as yet, to buy himself a carriage, and they stood for a while at the back of the room.

It was Judith who saw them first, and she waved and beckoned to them to come join her, Rosalind, and Lady Stockton, but Timothy just gave a slight shake of the head. A moment later Rosalind turned around and Christopher saw her eyebrows rise as she looked questioningly at them. He smiled warmly at her and it was as if a candle had been lit inside of her, for she suddenly seemed to glow.

They waited where they were until the intermission was announced, and watched the trio approaching, but Lady Stockton was stopped by an old friend, so the young ladies came toward them alone.

"Why did you not join us?" Judith asked Lord Graystone. "We had kept seats for you, as you could clearly see."

Rosalind guessed the reason at once. "Papa forbade you to see me, didn't he?" she almost whispered.

"Not to see you exactly," Christopher corrected her gently, "but he made it clear that I am not welcome in your home for the time being."

"But that is nonsense. Papa would never do something like that," Judith declared, then realized from the look on her sister's face that it was quite true. "But surely it does not apply to you also, Lord Graystone, does it?"

His smile was gentle, but he said firmly, "I will not go where my brother is not welcome, my dear."

Lady Stockton, who had kept a careful eye upon her daughters, could not help hearing the last remarks as she came toward them. "Too much is being made of this, particularly in such a public place," she said in a quiet but decided tone. "Why don't you gentlemen join us for refreshments and we can, perhaps, talk about it later somewhere more private than at an occasion of this sort."

Lord Graystone bowed and then stepped back to let the ladies go ahead of them. He raised his eyebrows slightly to his brother, who nodded, and the two of them brought up the rear. They could hear Lady Stockton speaking softly but urgently to her daughters but could not, of course, catch more than an odd word here and there.

The ladies went directly to a small table that was still available, while the gentlemen went over to the buffet table and secured a selection of delicacies first, then returned to procure tea for the ladies and a glass of wine each for themselves.

While at the buffet table, there had been little opportunity for private conversation, but Christopher had asked his brother, once again, if he was really sure he wanted to stop calling at the Stockton's home, for it was not at all necessary for him to do so.

"To me it is," Timothy replied. "It's a matter of principle and family, and on this we should most decidedly stand firm."

Though Christopher accepted this with a smile and a shrug, he meant to go into it further with him at some more opportune time and place. He was actually finding Lady Stockton's obvious embarrassment most amusing, and wondered how she was going to cope with the rather stilted conversation that would now inevitably take place. He felt sure he could prevent any outburst from Rosalind with just a glance, but doubted that his brother had as yet reached that stage of familiarity and trust with Judith.

There was a rather ominous silence when the two gentlemen brought the beverages and took their seats, not by the side of, but across from each of their ladies.

Once he was comfortably settled, Christopher looked over at Rosalind, who had not taken her eyes from his face since he had reached the table. He gave her what he hoped was a reassuring smile, and, after a moment, she managed something that was but a shadow of her usual response. Slowly, while a twinge of amusement played around his mouth, he lowered one eyelid, and at last received from her the wide, generous smile to which he was accustomed.

He breathed a sigh of relief, for he knew now that she would trust him and would not say or do anything to make the situation worse than it already was.

"I really did not expect you gentlemen to attend this evening," Lady Stockton began, "for music has usually little appeal to menfolk, whether young or old. As you have no doubt already guessed, it has been many years since I was able to prevail upon Lord Stockton to escort us to a musicale such as this. But my dear Judith assured me that you had promised to be here, and insisted that we save places for you."

She was addressing Lord Graystone, but allowed her glance to fall casually over Mr. Ferguson also.

"Having promised, we would not have dreamed of staying away, Lady Stockton."

It was Lord Graystone who responded, but he turned to his

brother for a moment, as though to make sure she was fully aware that he was speaking for both for them.

Christopher took a plate of pastries and offered it to Rosalind for her selection, looking at her intently all the while. She chose a creamy confection, picking it up and taking a delicate bite, then running her tongue slowly over her lips to remove the excess cream that had lodged there. As she did so, she never took her eyes from his, and he felt a sudden rush of warmth and a decided discomfort in his lower regions.

He was quite certain that she did not realize the devastating effect it had upon him, and he looked forward to the day—or more probably the night—when he might thoroughly explain the matter to her.

Judith's rather shrill voice broke through their spirit of communion.

"But you promised a week ago that you would call and take us to the balloon ascension, my lord." She pouted, then was silenced not by her mama's quelling glance, but by the look of warning that Lord Graystone gave her.

Rosalind reached out a hand to firmly clasp that of her sister. Then she said quietly, "Don't let the whole *ton* realize our papa's folly, Judith. We'll talk about this when we get home."

Lady Stockton's face had at first shown relief when she realized that Rosalind could handle the matter best, but she now glared at her older daughter, though in the present company she did not dare take it further.

"Will you sit with us when the music resumes?" Judith asked. "Or is that no longer allowed?"

"I'll sit with you, my dear, provided my brother may do so also," Graystone said gently, looking at Lady Stockton who nodded, seeming, for once, to be in a situation that she simply could not control, and when they returned to their places a few minutes later she made no demur when Ferguson took a seat beside Rosalind.

The seats were, unfortunately, placed several inches apart,

so there was no possible way for even shoulders to touch, but suddenly Rosalind could feel Christopher's leg against her own, as it had been during that special dinner, and she felt at least a temporary security.

It lasted, however, only until the brothers handed them into their carriage that evening, and then she felt completely bereft.

Unfortunately, their papa was not at home when they reached the house in Upper Brook Street, and there was, therefore, no opportunity to question him, so she excused herself and retired at once.

Her mama, quite obviously relieved that she did not intend to make a scene, hurried to her bedchamber, with Judith hot on her heels.

Though she knew that it would achieve nothing, Rosalind still cried herself to sleep that night, and she opened her eyes the next morning to a feeling of utter desolation even before she remembered the reason why.

Chapter Ten

Rosalind found her papa in the breakfast room, immersed in his morning newspaper—not the best time, she knew, to interrupt him. Nevertheless, she meant to find out just what he had said to Christopher.

"I'll have a piece of ham and a poached egg," she told Walters, "and a hot cup of tea, please."

Fresh toast was on the table, so she helped herself to a piece and spread it generously with butter.

Lord Stockton had peered at her from around the edge of his newspaper when she first entered the room, and given a grunt in response to the brightest "Good morning," she could muster, and he was now once more completely hidden from her view behind the paper.

"I came down early so that I might have a word with you, Papa, before anyone else is here to interrupt us," she told him, then waited to see if the newspaper would move in the slightest.

"Can't it wait until later in the day?" Lord Stockton snapped. "You know quite well that I dislike being disturbed at this hour."

"But this is of the utmost importance," she told him, not willing to be put off so easily.

"I'm sure it must be very important to you, if it caused you to get up at this hour," he said grimly, looking over the top of the newspaper so that she could see only his bushy iron gray brows, blue eyes paler than her own and now a little watery, and the top half of his cheeks and nose.

When she was not intimidated but stared straight back at him, he finally lowered the newspaper and asked, "What is it that you want? An advance on next month's allowance?"

"You know quite well, Papa, that it's not me but Judith who always spends everything at once," she replied, giving way to her impatience. "What I would like to know is just what you said to Mr. Ferguson to make him believe that he is not welcome to call here anymore."

"I do not at all like your attitude, young lady," Lord Stockton said sternly, "and I would suggest that you go back to your bedchamber and see me in my study in a couple of hours. It is my hope that by then you will feel more like addressing me with some of the respect due to your father."

He buried himself once more in his newspaper and Rosalind really could not blame him, for she knew that she was at fault in speaking to him in such a way.

Leaving her breakfast untouched, she rose. "I'm sorry and I do beg your pardon, Papa," she said quietly. "I will come to your study at eleven o'clock, if I may."

His response was one more grunt, and she had no idea that his brevity had been absolutely necessary. Had he started to say more he would have been forced to take her in his arms and comfort her, for he could hear the unshed tears in her voice. He could not help himself, but he had always loved her more than either of his other daughters. He tried not to show it, and for that reason he was inclined to be a little too harsh with her at times.

She went slowly up the stairs and back to her chamber, turning the key in the lock in case Judith should, by some strange chance, be awake and decide to come in and talk about last evening.

Both her mama and her sister tapped lightly on her door, but she did not hear them and would have ignored them in any case. Even when Molly, the chambermaid, knocked and called softly, she did not answer at first. Then she realized that the girl would be behind in her work for the rest of the day if she did not let her in, so she crossed the room and allowed her to enter. There was still ten minutes to go before she could see her papa once more.

"Is there anything I can do for you, Miss Rosalind?" she asked. "Get you a cup of tea or something?"

Rosalind smiled weakly and shook her head. "No, thank you, Molly. I'm going down to see Papa in just a few minutes now," she said.

Moving slowly over to the pier mirror, she carefully checked her appearance, noting that she looked a little pale, but there was not much she could do about that at the moment. Eleven o'clock of a morning was hardly a good time to dip into the rouge pot, and that was the only thing that would have helped.

Bracing her shoulders, she gave the girl a bright smile, then walked swiftly across the room and down the stairs.

In response to her light rap on the door, Lord Stockton called for her to enter, but he looked stern as he motioned for her to take a seat across from his desk.

"Now, young lady," he said, "What is all this about?"

"As Mama has probably told you," she started, "we saw Lord Graystone and Mr. Ferguson last evening, and they told us that, at your request, they would no longer be calling at this house."

"It was never my intention that Lord Graystone stay away," he said, frowning, for this had definitely not been what he expected, and it posed quite a problem, "but I did suggest that Mr. Ferguson refrain from calling here for now, to give you the opportunity to meet other gentlemen."

"I have had more than a year to meet other gentlemen, Papa," Rosalind pointed out quietly, "and the only gentleman I have ever had the slightest interest in is Christopher Ferguson. I was not aware that he had asked for my hand."

"He hasn't yet." Lord Stockton looked embarrassed, then he added in an exasperated tone. "Your mama and I are concerned that you might turn into another Lady Holland, and would prefer that you found a husband more suited to your station in life. Young Ferguson does not appear to be in a position to support a wife, and we have no wish for you to marry a penniless politician so very much beneath you.

"I'll not deny that I like him, for he has a good head on his shoulders, but he needs to seek an heiress who can give him good standing and financial help. I told him as much."

When he spoke of Lady Holland, Rosalind suddenly realized what this was all about and, for the second time that day, forgot to control her tongue. "And do you mean to sacrifice Judith also, for no reason other than that our dear mama has taken Lady Holland in dislike?" she asked angrily.

"Just you watch your tongue, young lady," Lord Stockton said sternly. "How dare you speak of your mama in such a tone. You're not too old to receive a thrashing for your impertinence, you know. Until further notice you are not to leave this house unless you are in the company of another member of the family, and if I hear that you have been making any secret assignations with Ferguson, you will be sent back to the country for the remainder of the Season. And now you may go to your room and stay there."

Looking not at all repentant, but angry beyond words, Rosalind turned around and left the study. She marched up the stairs with her head held high, and went directly to her chamber where she was gratified to find that the maid had finished her chores and left.

She was too furious for tears now, and hoped that her mama would not come near her for some time, for she was not sure that she could be as circumspect as she needed to be with the one person who, she felt, was the cause of all her problems.

The restrictions her father had imposed meant little to her, for she had no desire to go out at all if she was not permitted to meet with Christopher when she did so.

She reached for the book she had started to read a few days ago, then flung herself into a chair and leafed through the pages until she found where she had left off. Perhaps Jane Austen could make her feel a little calmer of spirit, but she very much doubted it.

A couple of hours later, after reading the same chapter over and over again without having the slightest recollection of what it was about, she hurled the book across the room just as the door opened and Peter came in.

He looked at the book that had so narrowly missed his head, then said, "Your aim seems to be off a little, Ros. Want me to toss it back to you and see if you can do better next time?"

"No, of course not," she said irritably, for the first time that morning very close to tears. "Do come in and sit down, but I must warn you that I'm in the most dreadful of moods right now."

"What's going on around here?" Peter asked, once he was comfortably settled on the bed. "I understand that Papa and Mama had a tremendous quarrel about a half hour ago, and it seems that you were the cause of it."

"If I was, it would be interesting to know which one was for me and which one against," Rosalind said dryly. "The last I heard they were in complete agreement in everything except where and when I should be hung, drawn, and quartered."

"That bad was it?" he asked sympathetically. "Is there anything I can do to help?"

She sighed heavily. "I wish there was, but as usual I brought much of it upon myself with my own wretched temper. I could hardly expect Papa to be at all lenient when I flew into a rage and said unpleasant things about Mama and her dislike of Lady Holland."

"And I suppose you said so much that he forbade you to see Ferguson for the present," Peter said, nodding.

"Oh, no," Rosalind said, "You've got it completely the wrong way round. It all started because he told Christopher Ferguson that he was not to call here for the time being. Apparently Mama was behind it, but she's been hoist with her own petard, for where his brother cannot go, neither will Lord Graystone."

Peter chuckled. "Not very well thought out, I would say," he remarked, "and that accounts for Judith having a fit of the sulks also. Are you on bread and water?"

Suddenly Rosalind realized that she had not eaten today as yet.

"So far, I'm not even on that, for I flung out of the breakfast room without touching my food, and I see it's now past lunch-time," she said, though she did not feel at all in need of sustenance.

"Do you want me to get you something?" Peter asked.

Rosalind shook her head. "I don't really want anything," she told him. "I'm sure something will be sent in this evening, if I'm not invited to sit at table. And, to be honest, I'd rather stay here than try to eat supper with everyone glaring at me, for I've no doubt at all that Judith will also blame me for what has happened. Any further transgression and I'm to be packed off to the country for the rest of the Season," she said, a disgusted look on her face.

"Oh, come on, Ros, that's ridiculous," Peter said, laughing. "Surely you're exaggerating?"

She shook her head. "That's exactly what he said; on my word of honor," she told him, placing her hand on her heart.

"That's utter nonsense, Ros," Peter said in disgust. "Do you want me to tell Ferguson or Graystone about it?"

She shook her head. "That's one of the transgressions he named. And, in any case, I don't really know if Chistopher feels as strongly as I do. He may think that the whole thing is more trouble than it's worth."

She turned away, unwilling to let her brother see the tears that, for the first time that day, filled her eyes and threatened to spill over.

Peter waited quietly until she was able to turn back to him. Then he got up and put an arm around her shoulder.

"Don't start thinking that. If he's not said anything it's probably because of the problems in France, and the fact that he'll be going over there as soon as it comes to a head. I've seen the way he looks at you, and Mama must have done so, also, or she wouldn't be so worried. I'm going out for a while, but I'll be back for supper and I'll make sure you get something to eat, one way or another.''

He gave her a warm hug before turning and leaving her bedchamber.

When he had gone, Rosalind suddenly felt very tired, possibly due to her lack of sleep last night, and she stretched out on top of the bed covers and lay there, resting and remembering. She could vividly recall that first time when she and Christopher had met in the conservatory, just as if it was but yesterday, and the memory gave her the strength and comfort she needed so badly.

She would not let herself believe that all that waiting had been in vain, she decided. Surely their meeting again, more than a year later, meant that it was right, and that they would be together eventually.

On that hopeful note she fell asleep and did not waken until several hours later when the sun was well past its zenith, and her stomach was starting to tell her that she needed food. It was not urgent, however, and she knew that if no one else took the trouble, Peter would see that she got something here in her chamber.

She still hoped that she would not be required to go down to dinner, for it would be an unpleasant meal at best, and she would much rather have something up here.

But it was not her brother, but Molly who came up more than an hour later with a tray of food.

''Cook said I was to bring this up, Miss Rosalind,'' the girl said, ''but even if she hadn't I meant to, for you've not eaten anything all day.''

It was more than obvious that she would have liked to criticize Lord and Lady Stockton, but dared not do so in case it got back to them and she was let go on the spot.

''Did she do this on her own?'' Rosalind asked. ''Or was it on Mama's instructions?''

''Perhaps her ladyship expected you to join them, Miss Rosalind,'' the maid said kindly. ''They only just started to eat.''

When the girl had gone she lifted the covers and found that

Cook had been more than generous, for there was a bowl of soup, sliced chicken with peas and potatoes, and a good sized piece of apple pie. There was also a glass of wine and a pot of tea for later.

Downstairs, the vacant chair where Rosalind usually sat seemed to demand that Peter say something, and finally, when he realized she must not have been told that she might come down to dine, he could keep quiet no longer.

"You know, Papa," he began, "that Rosalind often speaks first and regrets it afterward, and she would be the first to admit that she occasionally goes too far. But do you really think she should be confined to her chamber without any food all day? She's not a child anymore."

"What are you talking about, my boy?" Lord Stockton asked. "I gave no orders that meals should not be sent up to her." He turned to his wife. "Did you not make arrangements for Rosalind when you spoke with Cook this morning, my dear?"

"I did not see Cook until almost noontime," Lady Stockton said, "and when she told me that Rosalind had neglected to plan any of our meals for the day, a task she had been performing now for more than a year, I decided it would be good for her to do without. She should have seen Cook before she went up to her chamber."

"I was not aware that Rosalind was forced to take care of any of the household duties," Lord Stockton said quietly.

Lady Stockton looked a little embarrassed. "I have always felt that a girl should learn all such duties in preparation for when she has to manage a household of her own," she asserted, "and Rosalind is completely capable, at this point, of running this place singlehanded if necessary."

"I've no doubt that is excellent training," Lord Stockton agreed, "but surely there was no reason to penalize her for being unable to perform one of your own duties, my love. Did you not know that she did not have breakfast this morning because she was too upset to eat it?"

"Cook said something about it, but it was her own fault if

she did not eat it. No one stopped her from doing so, did they?'' she asked.

Putting down his knife and fork, he rose. ''Would you excuse me. I mean to see how she is without delay.''

Rosalind supposed the knock on the door to be her brother, and called for him to come in, but when her father entered, she immediately put down her knife and fork and looked at him rather guiltily.

''Ah, I see that Cook has more sense than I realized. I suppose she sent luncheon up to you also?'' he suggested.

Rosalind shook her head. ''No, Papa, she did not, and please do not blame her for sending supper up to me. She was only being kindhearted.''

He sat down on the edge of the bed and looked at her intently. Finally he said, ''You are not a little girl to be sent to bed without your supper, my dear. I am afraid it was a misunderstanding between me and your mama, and it will not happen again. Would you like to come down and join us now?''

''Would you mind awfully if I didn't, Papa?'' she asked. ''I'm sure Mama will not yet have forgiven me, and I'd rather not have her scold me also.''

A twinkle came into his eyes. ''Very well, but I want to talk to you again, so perhaps you could come down to the study when I have my port and cigar. And we'll both keep our tempers in check this time, won't we?''

She nodded. ''As soon as I hear you go through, I'll come down,'' she said.

He left then to resume his dinner, and Rosalind finished hers. She was not at all concerned now, for she knew her papa well enough to know that he meant what he said—he just wanted to talk to her.

It was almost an hour later that she joined him, and he motioned her to come and sit with him beside the fire this time.

If she had held the hope that he would change his mind and allow Christopher to come to the house again, she would have been disappointed, but she knew him far too well for that. The conversation they had was simply to reestablish the warm father and daughter relationship which they had always enjoyed. He told her how he had always been very proud of her, of her scholastic achievements, her integrity, and of the fine young woman she had become.

She, in turn, told him how much she loved him, even when she disagreed with his views, and begged that he would forgive her if she did things sometimes of which he did not approve. It was just about as far as she dare go in indicating that she was determined to eventually marry the man she loved—provided he still wanted her, of course.

In the days ahead she was irritated by the ban on her going out with just a maid, but her mama made sure that it was upheld. Rosalind even went so far as to write a note to Christopher, and she kept it in her reticule in the hope that she might meet him, or someone who knew him and could give it to him. She would not ask her brother to do so, for she did not wish to get him into trouble if he should be caught.

She had put aside her pride and expressed her feelings as far as she was able, telling him that she had never felt anything at all for the many other young men she had met. She made it clear that if he should feel the same way, and could let her know, she would simply wait for him until he was free of his commitment to Wellington and could come for her. A note addressed to her maid, Hetty, she told him, and handed to a groom, would reach her without fail. All she had to do now was find someone outside the family who would deliver it.

A few days later, when she was out with Peter and one of his friends, she met Georgina Walters, the red-haired young lady who had been present at the Hollands' dinner. Miss Walters was with an acquaintance of Peter's, and they stopped to talk for a few minutes.

By chance, the subject of ices was mentioned, and Miss Walters remarked upon how very much she enjoyed the ones at Gunter's, but that she seldom went there. Suddenly Rosalind had a wonderful idea. "Why don't we all go there tomorrow afternoon?" she suggested, and the others readily agreed.

They met in the early afternoon, and while the gentlemen went to get the ices, Rosalind asked a favor of Miss Walters. "I wonder if you might be willing to do something for me," she said softly. "Mr. Ferguson and I are unable to see each other for the time being, and I hoped that you might be able to give him a note I have written."

"I'd be very happy to do so," Miss Walters said eagerly. "He's been grouchy ever since you stopped seeing each other, and if it will make him any sweeter tempered, I, for one, shall be most thankful."

Quickly, before the gentlemen came back, she took the letter that Rosalind held out and slipped it into her reticule.

"You need have no worries about its safe delivery," Miss Walters said. "I will give it to him this very afternoon as soon as I return to Holland House."

There had been a strange smile on the young lady's face, however, which worried Rosalind a little, for it had been impossible not to notice how much of the time her gaze had seemed fixed on Christopher when they had dined at the Hollands' home.

Miss Walters was certainly not the most suitable of messengers, for there was something about her that Rosalind could not like, but meeting her had seemed most opportune, and such a chance might not occur again for some time.

Chapter Eleven

When Georgina Walters returned to Holland House, she was careful to avoid the main rooms from which she could hear the sound of voices, for she had no wish for anyone to know she was back as yet. But as soon as she reached her bedchamber she could contain her excitement no longer and could hardly wait to take off her pelisse, bonnet, and gloves before tearing open the envelope that contained Miss Marshall's letter to Christopher Ferguson.

"Silly chit," she muttered, as she quickly scanned the letter that had taken Rosalind such a very long time to compose. "She doesn't have the sense to realize that he'll never be hers, for I've known he was mine since the first time I set eyes on him."

She was surprised to discover that the writing was in a much more practiced and elegant style than was usual for a lady, and this was a disappointment, for it would take much more time to copy, and she would need to get started right away.

Had she but known that Christopher had never seen Rosalind's penmanship, she could have saved herself some work for it took her the best part of an hour before she was successful in composing and carefully writing a new letter with which to replace Miss Marshall's.

The new one read:

My dear Christopher,

   I am writing to tell you that I have fallen in love at last.
I did not mean to do so, for I was quite sure that what you
and I felt for each other would eventually surmount Papa's
disapproval.

   I first met my love long before I met you, in fact it was
almost a year ago, and when Papa brought him to see me
again I knew that he was doing it only for the best.

   As the betrothal has not yet been officially announced,
I cannot reveal the name of my future husband, but you will
know of him soon enough and, I trust, give us your blessing.
Fondest wishes,
Rosalind

   She carefully read the letter to make sure that in her endeavor
to get the penmanship perfect she had not omitted any words.
Then she placed the note in an envelope, wrote Christopher's
name on the outside, and sealed it in much the same fashion
the original letter had been sealed. It was not the identical paper,
as Miss Marshall's had been written on a particularly fine
quality, but she felt sure that Christopher would be none the
wiser.

   Though she knew she should destroy Miss Marshall's letter,
she could not bring herself to do so. Instead, she placed it with
her own first effort, in her usual hand, and slipped both pieces
of paper under the lining of a drawer.

   When she opened the door to her bedchamber and listened,
she was relieved that she could still hear Christopher's voice
quite clearly, coming from the direction of Lord Holland's
study. It was as if the gods were on her side, so she moved
quickly but quietly down the hall to his bedchamber and stepped
inside, pausing for just a minute to be sure no servant was there.

   A moment later she placed the envelope in the center of his
small desk, then hurried out of the bedchamber. She was only
just in time, for as she quietly closed the door of her own
chamber, she heard voices and footsteps as he came up the stairs
in the company of one of Lord Holland's guests.

She heard the door to his bedchamber close quietly, and the other man's footsteps continue along the hall, then there came the sound of Christopher's door slamming hard, and heavy footsteps hurrying along the corridor and going down the stairs at a rapid pace. Startled, for this was not what she had expected, she rushed out of her room, and was just in time to see Christopher fly out of the front door as if the devil himself was after him.

This was a most unsatisfactory development, but she dare not have gone after him, even if she had known where he had gone to. Perhaps his haste had nothing to do with the letter, she thought, and entered his chamber once more. Nothing was disturbed inside to give her even an inkling of why he had left in such haste, but when she looked at the desk, the letter was no longer in sight.

Christopher paid off the hackney and ran up the steps of Number Six, Upper Brook Street. He was pleased to note that the footman showed not the slightest reluctance to allow him inside, so at least he had not been told to refuse him admission.

"If Lord Stockton is at home, please tell him that I would like to have a word with him," he told the man, who looked only mildly surprised that he had neither hat, cane, nor even gloves with him. "I'll wait here," Christopher added.

A moment later the footman returned looking most apologetic. "I'm sorry, sir," he said, "but his lordship has not yet returned from his tailor. If you—"

Before he had a chance to say more, Rosalind came out of the drawing room and, without a moment's hesitation, started toward him.

"Papa's still not home, but it should not be very long now before he returns. Won't you come inside and I'll send for a fresh spot of tea and something to nibble upon while you wait for him?" she suggested. "Mama has just gone up to change for dinner, but I can ask Judith to join us."

"What I have to say to both you and him needs to be done in private," he told her angrily. "I'll—"

"Then why don't we go into the garden before anyone hears you and tries to stop us," she suggested, taking his arm and leading him toward the service door. "Mama may be down very shortly, and if she sees us she's bound to object to our being alone together, even in the hall."

He shook her hand off as though it were distasteful, and she gave him a look of surprise, then shrugged slightly and picked up a shawl that had been left on the hall table earlier in the day. Slipping it around her shoulders, for the late afternoons were often cool outdoors, she led the way past the kitchens and out through the back door.

When they reached a bench that was quite hidden from any of the lower windows, she sat down at one end, then turned to face him. "I would strongly recommend that you take a seat also, for you're very tall, and I cannot guarantee that your head might not be seen from one of the bedroom windows."

He did as she suggested, but sat as far away from her as possible, and Rosalind could not help but wonder if he might not fall off altogether were he to inch himself any further away from her. And, in all honesty, she almost wished that he would, for he was being unreasonably cross with her.

"Are you angry because I wrote to you?" she asked. "I know it was most forward of me to do so, but I could not help myself. I simply had to tell you how I felt."

"About your future husband?" he asked, glaring at her quite furiously. "It didn't take you very long to find someone else, did it? But no, I forgot, he was waiting in the wings all the time, wasn't he?"

She frowned, wondering what he could possibly be talking about, and then gave him a puzzled look, but decided it was best to say nothing and hope to find out eventually what this was all about.

"On the last occasion that I spoke with your father, he gave me his word that he would inform me well in advance of any pending betrothal," he said sharply. "I can only think now that he lied to me, for if this happened so quickly afterward, it seems to me that the gentleman must have already made his feelings known before I was asked to discontinue calling.''

"And I can only think that either you or I must be a candidate for Bedlam," Rosalind said thoughtfully, "for I have not the slightest idea what you are talking about."

"Do you deny that you wrote this letter to me?" he asked, withdrawing the envelope from his pocket and waving it in front of her face.

"That I wrote to you I do not for a moment deny," she said, frowning as she caught a glimpse of the cheap quality of the paper, "but I certainly did not write that letter, for the paper is very much inferior to the kind we use."

Christopher's eyebrows rose and it was his turn to look puzzled.

"Come to think of it, I did feel it was rather odd that you should say you'd known him much longer than you'd known me, when it had been only a year," he said thoughtfully. "Here, take a look at it."

She reached out and took the envelope he handed to her, turning it over and noticing that though the writing resembled hers, it was much heavier, and the ink was darker also.

Sliding the sheet of paper out, she unfolded it and stared at it, a look of complete consternation on her face. "This is not the letter I wrote to you," she told him quietly. "I suppose I should have known better than to trust Miss Walters, but I had written it, then carried my letter around for several days, and seeing her seemed like a wonderful opportunity. Did she hand it to you in person?"

He shook his head, smiling a little grimly. "I have not the least idea how it got there, but it was in my bedchamber when I went back upstairs this afternoon. I took a hackney and came over here right away."

"I'm extremely glad you did, for it had occurred to me that Miss Walters might not do as she had promised, but I had to take the chance." A dreadful thought seemed to suddenly strike her. "Have you, perhaps, been paying her some attention since Papa would not allow you to see me?"

"Rosalind!" Christopher said sharply. "You surely cannot believe that I would behave in such a way?"

She shook her head. "I have to admit that I don't know what to believe, for you've never told me, in so many words, just how you feel about me, though we have teased each other about it at times."

"I was trying to behave honorably," he said quietly. "Until I am in a position to offer marriage, I did not think it quite the thing to tell you outright how strongly I feel about you. But that did not mean that I did not love you with all my heart. I thought you understood that."

"I needed reassurances," she said softly. "The letter I wrote to you expressed my feelings as far as I was able, and asked you to let me know if you felt the same way. If so, I wrote that I would gladly wait for you, however long it might be, but I needed to be assured that I was not waiting in vain."

Something in his gaze told her all she needed to know, and she might have flung herself into his arms were it not for the sound of footsteps hastening toward them from the direction of the house.

A moment later, Lord Stockton confronted them.

"What is the meaning of this?" he demanded angrily. "I thought you were a man of honor, sir, and did not think you would go behind my back and meet with my daughter, not even in my house, but in the privacy of this deserted garden."

Christopher had risen respectfully when Lord Stockton appeared, and now he showed him the letter which had purported to come from Rosalind.

"I received this, sir, and thought you had gone back on your word," he said stiffly. "I came here to confront you with it, but in your absence I confronted your daughter instead."

"This is not at all Rosalind's style," Lord Stockton said slowly, after reading it carefully. "Nor is it her writing, though it is quite similar. I cannot blame you for wishing to see me with this, but you now know, I am sure, that the contents are quite fictitious."

"Yes, sir, I do. And after my conversation with Rosalind this afternoon I would like to ask you to reconsider your decision that we not see each other for the time being," Christopher said. "We neither of us fare well apart, and though I lack the title you would, of course, much prefer, I am not quite in such impecunious circumstances as you seem to believe. My father had a good head for business, and most of his fortune, which was extremely well invested, was left to me, though I have not felt the need to touch it as yet. I believe it is my mama's intention to divide the portion my father left her between any daughters I may produce."

Lord Stockton glared at him then grunted in disgust. "Why could you not have told me this when we discussed the matter before."

A half smile flickered across Christopher's face. "Because I was not then asking you for Rosalind's hand in marriage, my lord. Now I am, but I would prefer the wedding to take place after our final battle with Napoleon."

"Do you think you can handle her?" Lord Stockton asked, a little grimly. "She's always been the most unbiddable of all our daughters, you know."

Christopher looked at Rosalind, who suddenly seemed to glow with happiness. "I think we can handle each other, my lord," he said softly, without taking his eyes away from her lovely face.

"Very well. You have my blessings, and I know that Lady Stockton will also be pleased, for the last couple of weeks have not been very peaceful ones in this household."

Rosalind was on her feet in a moment, throwing her arms around her father and hugging him tight. "Thank you, Papa. I know that you'll not regret this, and that you'll bring Mama around to your way of thinking."

She stepped back then, and slipped her hand into that of her betrothed.

As if conjured up by her daughter's remark, Lady Stockton suddenly appeared at her husband's side. "Good evening, Mr. Ferguson," she said, her gaze going at once to the clasped hands. "I'm afraid no one had the forethought to inform me that you had called. Will you join us for dinner?"

"Thank you, my lady," Christopher said, completely ignoring her pointed glance. "But I must regretfully decline for, as you see, I am not dressed for the occasion. I'm afraid that in my haste to straighten out a most unfortunate misunderstanding, I completely forgot the time of day."

"Are congratulations in order, my dear?" Lady Stockton asked her husband.

"Yes, my love," he told her firmly. "I believe that it would be a grave injustice to keep these two young people apart any longer. I shall, of course, see that the necessary announcements go out, and I believe that a conventional courtship of about three months will enable them to get to know each other better. I'm sure that you and Rosalind will be able to work out the details."

"A courtship of three months at the very least is necessary," Lady Stockton said in some alarm, "for I'm not at all sure that I can see Judith through the rest of the Season and complete all the arrangements for a wedding in so short a time. Would you prefer to be married at St. George's in Hanover Square, or in the country, my dear Rosalind?"

"Oh, in the country, of course, and as simple a wedding as possible, Mama," Rosalind said at once. "I'd prefer the minimum of fuss, and as the date will depend entirely upon the progress of Napoleon Bonaparte, I do not believe that the exact time can be decided for now."

She turned toward Christopher to seek his agreement, and he smiled at her encouragingly.

Suddenly she felt incredibly shy, something she had not experienced since the early months of her first come-out. It was all the more surprising to her that she felt so willing to agree to whatever arrangements Christopher might suggest. However, she could not help but doubt that this situation would pertain for long, for she knew it was not in her nature to accept another's judgment without question.

There was a sound of hurried footsteps and then Judith came into view. The sight of Rosalind's happy face, and Christopher still clasping her hand, made her pause for a moment, and then she came forward eagerly.

"It is settled, then?" she asked. "Have Mama and Papa agreed that you may see each other again?"

"The announcement of the betrothal will not be made until tomorrow," Lady Stockton told her, "so don't you go telling any of your friends about it this evening. I'd not like a rumor to go around before it is official."

"But it means that Lord Graystone will be able to call on us again, doesn't it?" Judith said a trifle too eagerly for her mama's liking, for she frowned her displeasure at her younger daughter.

"I am sure he will wish to offer his best wishes to Rosalind, and let people know that he is most happy about his brother's choice of a bride," Lady Stockton said firmly. "And it will, of course, be quite proper for him to join our party again when next we visit Almack's."

Forgetting her recent feelings of displeasure with her sister, Judith flung herself into Rosalind's arms and hugged her, then she offered her hand to Christopher who bowed low over it.

"It will be marvelous to have you as a brother-in-law, and I know you'll make Rosalind very happy," she told him, almost as excited about the betrothal as her sister. "You're quite perfect for each other, you know."

"If we cannot prevail upon you to stay for supper with us, my boy, won't you at least come inside and allow us to drink a toast to you both?" Lord Stockton asked, smiling benignly. "I believe Walters always keeps a bottle of champagne cooling for just such an occasion."

When Christopher agreed, Lord and Lady Stockton, with Judith, led the way toward the house, while Rosalind and Christopher brought up the rear. When they had to stop to disentangle Rosalind's shawl from an encroaching hedge, Christopher took the opportunity to ask her if she was really quite sure that this was what she wanted.

"I don't want all the fuss and palaver that comes with announcements in the papers, if that's what you mean," she said with a heavy sigh, "and I'm much afraid that Mama will want to give us an engagement party before long. But I do want us to get married, and the sooner we can do so, the happier I will be.''

There was a new warmth in his eyes that made her feel strangely giddy, and when his arm slid around her shoulders as he was putting her shawl back in place, she did not try to move away, but waited patiently for the touch of his lips against her own.

This time his kiss was different from the last one, so very long ago, for there was nothing demanding about it. Rather it was a gentle affirmation of the agreements they had just made and, as it strengthened, a promise of the love that would hold them together through the arduous months and years that lay ahead.

They had already drawn apart and were proceeding once more along the narrow footpath when Lady Stockton came back to look for them. She eyed them with a great deal of suspicion, but there was nothing she could accuse them of without proof.

''From now on it won't do at all for the two of you to be alone like this, and I shall make sure that one of us is with you at all times, for the wedding is sudden enough without giving people cause to talk,'' she told them sharply. ''I must put you both on your honor that you will behave circumspectly, for we have never had so much as a hint of scandal in our family.''

''The only thing I'll promise, my lady,'' Christopher said, ''is not to do anything to Rosalind that will harm her in any way. But I have no doubt whatsoever, that when you and Lord Stockton were betrothed, you managed to have a modicum of privacy despite your parents' attempts to prevent it.''

He had quite obviously hit upon the truth, for she flushed and looked decidedly flustered.

''I'm afraid that is how Lord Stockton and I know what to expect of you,'' she said, smiling a little self-consciously. ''And in your case it is worse, for you will be going away and putting your life in danger before you get married, my dear Christopher. I will be frank and tell you that my daughter would never be able to hold her head up again—nor would any of us, for that matter—if you did not come back from the battle, and she found herself in a family way.''

''Mama, what a dreadful thing to say,'' Rosalind exclaimed.

Christopher was, however, a little more realistic—and more reassuring.

''I give you my word that such a thing will not happen, my lady,'' he said firmly. ''But I'll not say we won't try to be alone sometimes, for we'll need to be able to talk our plans over in privacy.''

With this, Lady Stockton had to be content, and she was left hoping that they would be as discreet as she and Lord Stockton had been.

Chapter Twelve

No amount of persuasion could convince Christopher to dine with the Stocktons that evening, dressed as he was, and he did, in fact, also miss dinner at Holland House, but as he had always been on the friendliest of terms with the kitchen staff, they made sure that a more than substantial supper was sent up to his office.

Afterward, he met with Lord and Lady Holland in private, and they were both delighted to hear of his betrothal. They had liked Rosalind very much and had suspected that romance was in the air there, though Lady Holland had thought Lady Stockton a whey-faced, hen-witted creature.

Christopher also told Lord Holland that he would be out for much of the next few days, but would catch up with his work in the evenings. That was completely satisfactory to Lord Holland, for their arrangements had ever been a very loose one, meant for the benefit of both.

His first visit the following morning was to Graystone House, which had, of course, been his home for many years and to which he was still an almost daily visitor when in town.

The family were all at breakfast, and another place was set at the table immediately, so that he might join them.

"To what do we owe such an early call, my boy?" Glastonbury asked. "I do not mean to imply that you're not most welcome here at any time of the day or night, as you well know, but it would seem to me that you must have urgent news to impart.''

"Let me guess,'' his brother said with a wide grin. "The Stocktons have at last approved of you as a future son-in-law. That's it, isn't it?''

Christopher nodded. "I meant to wait until I was a deal more sure of being in a position to marry Rosalind, with Napoleon put away for good and my future more settled, but I realized that it was grossly unfair to her to leave her wondering about my feelings.''

It was quite evident to all who saw the countess, that she must have been very beautiful as a young girl, for she was still lovely, though now nearing fifty years of age. The hair that had once been a light golden brown, was streaked with silver, and faint lines marred her pale complexion, but her eyes were just as bright a blue as ever.

She now looked considerably taken aback, for her boys, as she still thought of them, were not in the habit of telling her everything that went on between them.

"I cannot imagine why the Stocktons, or anyone else for that matter, could have the slightest objection to your marrying their daughter,'' she told her oldest son. "As you are determined to go actively into politics you'll probably always own little in the way of estates, but I've no doubt whatsoever that you'll have a knighthood before very long, and there's no knowing where you'll go after that.''

"Christopher has much of the stubborn Scottish pride in him, Mama,'' Timothy informed her. "He simply refused to tell Lord Stockton how he was financially placed until he was actually asking for Rosalind's hand, and her father was apparently worried that Christopher might be a penniless secretary for the rest of his life—in no position to support his daughter in the way to which she was accustomed. Then, of course, her mama is the type of woman who would always prefer a titled son-in-law to a plain mister.''

Christopher turned to his brother, his eyes twinkling with merriment. "I haven't told Lord Stockton any details even now, but I have indicated that my father left most of his moneys to me. I'm not at all sure that I will be able, or willing, to emulate Lord Stockton's standards, for I believe that along with my father's money, I inherited some of his Scottish thriftiness, and I'll not live high on the hog and be hopelessly in debt, as do as least half of the *ton*.''

"Does your affianced know that this is the way you feel?" his mama asked, a smile of genuine amusement on her face.

He looked startled, for the word *affianced* suddenly brought home to him the reason he had called so early this morning.

"Not at the moment, for we've had little chance to discuss such matters, but you may be sure that she soon will. With all the fussing, however, I completely forgot why I came here this morning, Mama, for I wanted to ask your advice," he told her. "How does one go about buying a ring? Is it normal to find out the young lady's preference, or does one rely on the jeweler to know what is suitable?"

The countess laughed at her son's naïveté. "If one relied on a jeweler for any sort of recommendation there's no doubt that he would make sure you came away with the most costly ring in the store, and your pockets quite empty. But fortunately there's no need for any of that, for I've been keeping the rings your father gave me when we married, for just such a time as this. You'll not be ashamed of them, I can assure you."

He gave her a curious look. "I suppose I was too young to have noticed your rings at that time, but I have a faint recollection of seeing an emerald, though in what form I have not the vaguest idea," he told her.

"Very good," she said, smiling and nodding to herself. "When we've finished breakfast I'll take you upstairs and show them to you. I don't know the Stocktons at all well, for we go so little into society these days, but I seem to recall a family of that name having an estate in Rutland County."

Christopher grinned. "That's right. In fact, that was where I first met Rosalind, when I was home recovering from the scratch, and Lord Holland took me up there to a christening, of all things."

"Then you've known her for quite a long time," the countess said, "for surely that must be a good deal more than a year ago."

"I'm afraid that I did not know who she was at the time, and I feared I had lost her completely. Then our dear Timothy found her for me again," he said, grinning at his brother and knowing quite well he had given his mama a puzzle that she would not leave alone until solved.

A few minutes later they went upstairs together, arm in arm. On entering her chamber, she took him over to an armoire, crouched down and unlocked a drawer hidden away in the back, then brought out a velvet box.

"Take a look," she suggested, "and tell me now if you can recall them."

He gasped when he opened the box for there were the two rings, one a gold wedding band studded with diamonds. The other, a gold betrothal ring, held a large, marquise-shaped emerald that would have attracted considerable attention in any setting, but surrounded as it was with glittering diamonds it quite took his breath away. He could see why, as a very small child, he had found it fascinating enough to retain a faint recollection of it all these years later.

"Surely you don't want to part with these, Mama," he said, turning to look at her in wonder as he saw tears in her lovely, expressive eyes.

"Of course, I do, for this is what I have saved them for all these years. Don't ever allow anyone to say anything bad about your father, Christopher. Though he was not high born, he was a very fine man, honest to a fault, and he would have been so proud if he could but see you now," she said, so softly that he had to strain to catch the words.

He put his arms around her and held her close, then, after a moment, she closed the box and pressed it into his hand.

"I've been very fortunate to have not one, but two such wonderful husbands, who gave me fine sons. I hope you'll do the same for this young lady, and I want to meet her as soon as possible. Do you think you could inquire of Lady Stockton what afternoon might be convenient for me to call? And now," she said, allowing him to help her to her feet, "take these, for if the announcement is going into the newspaper right away, Rosalind will want a ring to show to all of her friends who wish her happy."

"I'll bring her around to see you just as soon as we can arrange it, Mama," he told her warmly, slipping the box into his jacket pocket.

"Yes, and I will talk to Lady Stockton, when I see her, about a suitable date for us to give a dinner in your and Rosalind's honor." She smiled. "This is so very exciting! When do you mean to be married?"

"That now depends upon Mr. Bonaparte," Christopher said quietly. "I'll not marry until we've put him away once more, and for good this time."

She closed her eyes so that he could not see the pain in them, for she had, for the moment, forgotten that he meant to return to the Continent for what was thought of as the final battle. He did not hear the silent prayer she offered up, but he knew its content just the same.

Forcing a bright smile, she said, "Now, off with you, and make sure that your young lady has not changed her mind about marrying such a brave, foolish young man."

For a moment he looked unusually smug, for neither he nor Rosalind had any worries on that score, or so he thought.

His next visit was, of course, to Upper Brook Street, for he knew that the rings would burn a hole in his pocket until he gave them to Rosalind.

If Walters was surprised at so early a morning call, his face remained as impassive as ever as he took Christopher's hat and cane. "Miss Rosalind is, I believe, in the drawing room with Lady Stockton. If you will wait here for a moment, sir."

He was back almost at once, and showed him into the room with much more of a flourish than usual—or so it seemed—for the news of the betrothal had, of course, filtered down through the entire staff, with whom Rosalind was very popular.

"How very nice of you to call, Christopher," Lady Stockton

said, "and just at the right moment, for we were about to start making plans for the wedding. There is much to do in a very short time, you know."

"I have told Mama that we want as quiet a wedding as possible," Rosalind said to him, a look of appeal in her eyes, "but she still feels that we'll simply have to invite what seem to be a tremendous number of people whom I, for one, scarcely know."

"I have just come from Graystone House," Christopher told them both, "and my mama is most anxious to meet you, Rosalind, and, of course, to become acquainted with your mama and papa. She wondered what day would be convenient for her to call on you, Lady Stockton."

At the very idea of the countess calling upon her, Lady Stockton beamed. "Thursday would be quite convenient for me, if she would care to join us for tea, perhaps," she offered. "I'll just write her a note, if you would be good enough to take it to her."

She went over to an escritoire at once, and took out paper and pen.

This was an excellent opportunity for Christopher to give the rings to Rosalind, and he reached quickly into his pocket and brought out the box.

"My mother has been saving these, apparently, for my bride. I believe she would be most disappointed, but if you do not like them I can make other arrangements. They were the rings my father gave to her."

When he opened the box, Rosalind gasped, for though the wedding band was lovely, she was sure she had never seen anything quite so beautiful as the betrothal ring.

"I cannot imagine how anyone could possibly dislike them, Christopher," she said, feeling a little shy at this, his first gift to her. "I've always particularly liked emeralds, though I've never before owned one."

He took out the ring, the stones sparkling wonderfully in the sunlight shining in at the windows, then he reached for her left hand.

"If the fit is not right, they can, of course, be adjusted," he murmured as he slipped the ring onto her finger and moved it around to see if it was too loose.

"It's perfect in every way," she told him, and he lifted her hand to press his lips against the soft, white skin.

"What are you two whispering about?" Lady Stockton demanded to know, for Christopher's back was toward her and she could not see what was going on.

"Look, Mama, isn't it beautiful?" Rosalind said, a little breathlessly, as she went over to show off the ring.

Lady Stockton's eyes widened, then she looked across at Christopher. "Were they your mother's?" she asked.

He nodded. "My father gave them to her," he told her, "and she was apparently keeping them for this occasion. Surprisingly, although I was not much more than a baby when he died, I have a faint recollection of seeing the stone gleaming on her hand."

"Very lovely, and very suitable under the circumstances, my dear," she said to her daughter. "The wedding band will fit if this ring does. Let me just make sure that it's not too loose on your finger."

She reached out her hand to check, decided that it needed no adjustments whatsoever, then handed the wedding band back to Christopher. "You should keep this, for you'll need it on the day of the wedding."

He nodded. "I'm sure my mother will hold on to it for me, for I could easily lose it if I took it to the Continent," he said, slipping it back into his pocket. He smiled warmly at Rosalind, who was moving her hand around, enjoying the way the stone caught the rays of sunlight from the window.

There was the sound of footsteps hastening down the stairs, and then Judith came bursting into the room. She wished Christopher a good morning, then noticed the ring and hurried over to take a closer look at it.

"I've never seen one like it," she sighed, lifting her sister's hand and carefully examining the ring. "You'll be afraid of wearing it in case you lose it, I'm sure."

"No, I won't," Rosalind declared emphatically, "for I'll not take it off, or at least I'll not do so until Christopher puts the wedding band there.''

She looked across at him as she spoke, and experienced the oddest fluttering in her stomach and a strange feeling as though she could not quite catch her breath, for he gave her a most intimate smile that was meant for her alone, but which was closely observed by Lady Stockton.

Christopher remembered that his mother had very much wanted to meet Rosalind, but the fact that he did not own a carriage rather complicated this, for he could not invite her for a drive and then stop by Graystone House. There was a way, however, and he had not the slightest doubt that he could arrange it.

"My brother is most anxious to see Judith again," he told Rosalind. "If we call tomorrow afternoon, may we take you both for a drive?"

Before confirming it, Rosalind called to her sister, "Judith, would you like to take a drive tomorrow with Lord Graystone, Christopher, and me?"

For a moment her sister's eyes gleamed, then she put her nose high in the air and said, "I'm not sure that I want to see him again. After all, it was not I who decided we should stop seeing each other."

"Don't be ridiculous, child," Lady Stockton snapped. "It would have been most embarrassing for him to come here without Christopher, quite apart from the fact that I would not have liked the two of you to drive out frequently alone. Of course you must go with your sister tomorrow."

Judith shrugged. "Very well. If you say I must, Mama," she said, as if doing her mother a favor, but a gleam of excitement had returned to her eyes.

Promising to call, with his brother, the next afternoon, Christopher left then, and returned to Holland House, for he had not yet seen Georgina Walters to discuss the matter of the letters with her, and he did not mean to let her get away with such a despicable trick.

She had not been present when he had talked privately with

the Hollands last evening, and this morning he had left the house before anyone was down to breakfast. When he inquired of the butler as to her whereabouts, however, he was informed that Miss Walters had left the day before to visit some of her relatives outside of London, and would not be back for a few days.

As there was nothing to be done for now, he went to his own study and took care of a number of urgent matters for Lord Holland, so that he might be free tomorrow afternoon for the drive with Rosalind.

But when they set out the next afternoon, Christopher asked Timothy if he and Rosalind might be set down at Graystone House, for his mama would be home and he had told her that he would bring his betrothed to meet her.

They alighted and Christopher steered Rosalind through the front door. He gave his hat and cane to the butler, and they had just started toward the drawing room when the countess appeared in the doorway.

"Welcome, my dear," she said, drawing Rosalind close and pressing her cheek to that of her son's betrothed. Then she stepped back and took a good look at her. "You are almost exactly as I had imagined you would be."

But the countess was not at all as Rosalind had pictured her, for she was so very much younger looking, and seemed to be not at all high in the instep.

"Do come inside and we can have a most comfortable cose," she went on, directing Rosalind to a love seat in front of the hearth, then sitting down beside her.

Christopher strolled over to the bay window and stood looking out, a resigned expression on his face, for he knew that his mama would quickly set Rosalind at her ease, and they would start chattering away like a pair of magpies.

"The emerald looks quite perfect on your hand," the countess said, "and you have just the right coloring for it. You must tell me, though, if you do not like it, for I would not wish to force you to wear . . ."

Rosalind simply could not allow this lovely lady to think she did not like the loveliest piece of jewelry she had ever owned.

"How could I not simply love it?" she asked. "I have never seen anything to compare with it, and I shall treasure it always, I promise."

"And pass it along to your first son's wife, perhaps?" the countess asked, a twinkle in her eyes.

The thought of giving Christopher a son brought a rush of color to Rosalind's cheeks and she murmured, "Of course, my lady, but I hope to wear it myself for many happy years before doing so."

"Now, tell me how you are going to enjoy being the wife of a future prominent politician. I do hope that you are interested in the field of politics, for a fine hostess can considerably enhance a young man's chances." His mama gave Christopher a look of warm approval.

"I believe that I already know more about politics than do the majority of young ladies of my generation," Rosalind said proudly, "but I intend to apply myself even more, so that I can be of as much help to him as possible. That is, of course, if Christopher will allow me to do so."

"He will allow you to do anything you wish, within reason," Christopher called across from the window. "But you are not to even try to become a second Lady Holland."

The countess gave a little shudder. "I should think not, for you're not the type of person at all," she said. "And that does not mean that I do not admire Lady Holland, for I most certainly hold her in the highest esteem, but I would not like to see you emulate her or anyone else. Be an original, my dear. Let others hasten to copy you."

"Once I have learned more about Christopher's work and ambitions, I shall definitely try to do so," Rosalind said earnestly. "I just hope that he will be patient with me, and realize that I am trying very hard."

"He will. He's actually extremely patient," the countess said quietly. "And the other thing I meant to ask is if you have given any thought yet to where you would like to live? It might be better for you to rent a house in London until you are really sure of where you want to be. You would probably live in town a good deal of the year, of course, so it would need to be extremely comfortable.''

"Just as soon as we can, Mama, we mean to start looking for something suitable,'' Christopher called across. "I think that, for now, we'll try to find a house not far from Holland House, so that I can walk over there and back each day.''

"That's a good idea,'' Rosalind said, glad that he did not want her to stay with the Hollands, for she knew her mama would not like that at all. "And I would be able to go for walks in Kensington Gardens—with a maid, of course.'' She hastened to add the last words when she saw the frown that suddenly appeared on Christopher's brow.

This was the very first opportunity they had found in which they could discuss such practical matters, and Rosalind was glad to know that they were completely in agreement. It would always be like this, she decided, for they were so very much in love that they would quite naturally agree on all of the important things.

She had seen, of course, that her mama and papa quite frequently did not agree on many important matters, and though it sometimes seemed that her mama always got her own way in the end, she felt it was simply because her papa preferred not to put his foot down unless the issue at hand was something upon which he could not possibly compromise.

She and Christopher would not be at all like that, she knew, because they were so much closer in their thoughts and ideas.

"It's time that we were leaving, my dear,'' Christopher's voice broke through her thoughts. "Timothy and Judith will be here at any moment, and we would not wish to get you back too late for tea.''

"Of course,'' Rosalind said, turning to say her goodbyes to the countess. "It was so nice to meet you, my lady, and my mama asked me to tell you how very much she is looking forward to your visit. My sister, Judith, and I will both be there, of course.''

"Come along, Rosalind,'' Christopher said, steering her toward the door, "We mustn't keep them waiting, for I'm not at all sure Judith was prepared to forgive my brother just yet, and they may still be at loggerheads.''

"I know, for Judith still felt very hurt, but I'll warrant they have by now thrashed the matter out and that she has come around. My sister becomes hurt very quickly, but she also forgives and forgets just as fast. And it would seem that your brother is able to handle her a good deal more firmly than either Mama or Papa can.''

Rosalind was, of course, quite correct in her assumption, and when they stepped up into the carriage they found that all differences had been forgotten and Judith looked quite radiant once more.

Chapter Thirteen

It was when Rosalind and Christopher started to look for a house to rent that the question of moneys became a subject of grave concern between them, and it was, in fact, the very first serious matter upon which they had disagreed.

"This house is a little too large for our pockets. I believe we should try to be as thrifty as possible for the present," Christopher said, as the two of them went from room to room of a small mansion in Knightsbridge. "My father's money is invested in the Funds and I believe that, for now, we should be able to live comfortably enough on only a part of the income it produces."

Rosalind was fully aware of the fact that most gentlemen, her own father included, would not, as a rule, have ever dreamed of speaking of such matters to their wives, and even less would they have been a subject of discussion before marriage. But they were different, of course, for she knew that she could talk to Christopher about anything.

"I don't know what you mean by 'comfortably enough,' " she told him, "but we do not need to skimp, for I have a quite substantial dowry and also a generous portion which my Aunt Meg left me."

"If I could not support a wife, I would not have asked for your hand in marriage," Christopher said shortly, feeling not a little insulted. "The money you inherited from your aunt could be put to better use if invested and then passed on to our daughters. And your dowry should be held in trust, so that if something should happen to me, you would still be able to live comfortably."

"That is nonsense," Rosalind declared with a decided lack of discretion, but then discretion had never been her strong suit. "Part of the money my aunt left could provide dowries for our daughters, of course, but we could use the rest of it to make ourselves a little more comfortable in a larger house. And if you don't want to touch my dowry yourself, then I could use some of it instead of an allowance from you."

Christopher shook his head firmly. "What can we possibly need for the first year or so in the way of a house? We'll not be doing very much entertaining for some time, and a house this size would be far too big to keep up with the dozen servants I had in mind hiring to start with."

She laughed. "Did you ever stop and count the number of servants your mama has in town? I warrant you will find that she has at least thirty, not counting the grooms and stable boys, of course. In any case, servants don't cost much as long as you make sure they're not eating the same food as the family eats."

"My mama is married to an earl, and a wealthy one at that," Christopher said dryly. "And their town house has been owned by the earl's family for several generations. I would very much doubt that we will ever be in that position."

"I don't want to be in such a position," Rosalind asserted, "but I see no reason why we should not make use of whatever money we have available between the two of us. After all, that's what other people do."

He glared at her. "But we're not other people, Rosalind. If we want to be able to give our children a start in life, we cannot afford to live right up to the moneys we have coming in. If we did that, before you know it the price of something or other would go up and we'd be living above our means."

"That's the Scot in you talking," she declared. "Almost

everyone in London lives above their means, but no one thinks the worse of them for it.''

He was trying very hard to be patient with her, but finding it extremely arduous.

"Most of the people whom you know have prospects. They have parents who will be leaving money or estates to them when they pass on, my dear,'' Christopher tried to explain. "But I have already been left all that I am likely to get, and you cannot expect anything from your papa beyond your dowry, for in the normal course of events everything else will go to your brother.''

"But it's really six of one and a half dozen of the other,'' Rosalind argued, "for if you don't want to touch any of my money, and it is invested in the Funds for our children, we don't need to live on only the interest from your father's money. We could use some of it now.''

He sighed heavily. "Don't you see that if we look to rent a smaller house now, we'll be able to afford something larger when our children come along. I never pretended to be a tremendously wealthy man, Rosalind, but I can keep you in a reasonable amount of comfort for the rest of your days. Isn't that enough?'' he asked softly, placing a finger under her chin and looking earnestly into her eyes.

She nodded. "It's enough if I can just be with you,'' she whispered. "Let's not quarrel about it.''

He drew her into his arms and held her close, pressing his lips to her forehead. There was no doubt that the subject would come up again, but for now he felt he had made his point and that in time she would come to realize the wisdom of his words. Had he felt her to be a spendthrift, he would have been concerned, but he knew that much of the Stockton's house-keeping had been left in her hands, and that she was quite capable of running a home most economically.

"Have you two finished quarreling?'' Judith called up the stairs. She had been asked by her mama to accompany them today, and they had left her examining the collection of books

in the library while they went to look at the bedchambers.
"If you're making up, I promise to come up as slowly as I can,
but I am on my way."

They were forced to laugh, and Christopher dropped a kiss
on the tip of Rosalind's nose before releasing her, the problem
of moneys forgotten for the time being. Slipping an arm around
her waist he walked with her out of the master bedroom and
to the top of the stairs.

"I think we've seen as much of this house as we need," he
told Judith. "There's just one more on the list the agent gave
me. Can you put up with the pair of us for just a little longer?"

"Of course," she said. "You know I'd not have come upstairs
without warning you first. Is the one we've still to see as large
as this?"

"I don't think so," he said, frowning, "but we'll soon find
out, for it's only just around the corner."

He walked between the two young ladies as they stepped out
onto the street, searching for the last house on their list for the
day. To Christopher's relief, it was smaller than the others they
had seen that afternoon, but most attractive from the outside.
It would need a smaller staff, and the rental was considerably
lower as well.

"I like it," Judith said at once. "It has a welcoming look
about it, don't you think?"

"I'm not sure why," Rosalind murmured, experiencing a
feeling of relief, "but it's quite true. Don't you agree,
Christopher?"

"Yes, I do," he told her, nodding. "Let's take a look inside
though, before becoming too enthusiastic."

He turned the key in the lock and they walked into a small
but attractive hall with a drawing room, dining room, study,
and breakfast room leading off of it. A staircase curved
gracefully upward, and beneath it was the door to the kitchens
and servants' quarters in the back.

Glass panels on either side of the front door and a skylight
window high above, brought daylight into the hall.

They started their tour of inspection with the drawing room, and this time they stayed together as they roamed from room to room.

"I like it," Rosalind said decisively as they came out of the breakfast room and started up the stairs. "The rooms are smaller than the last house, but they're large enough, and it is so very much more warm and homelike."

Christopher nodded. "It's the best we've seen yet. I do hope that the bedchambers are not too small for comfort."

But they were just right. With the master suite and three additional chambers on the first floor, there was ample room. A quick inspection of the kitchens, pantries, laundry, and such, showed it to be a neat, compact home, with a butler's pantry, a housekeeper's sitting room, staff dining room, and bedrooms of various sizes for the servants.

"I should think this would suit," Rosalind said, "but I would still feel happier if we looked tomorrow at the rest of the ones offered, just to be sure we're making the right choice. Do you think they will hold this for us while we make up our minds?"

"I should think they'll be only too glad to do so," Christopher told her, "for there can be very few people looking for houses with the Season so well under way. I'll have a word with the agent in the morning."

It seemed to be a relief to both of them that they had been able to find something they agreed was most suitable without any further argumentation, and as they stepped into the Stockton's carriage, which had been borrowed for the day, no one would have believed that the young couple had ever had even the slightest disagreement.

Curious, however, after hearing them disagreeing earlier, Judith asked, "Don't you mind it in the slightest when Rosalind argues with you, Christopher? I cannot ever recall Mama speaking to Papa in such a way, but I suppose that they are just a little old-fashioned."

He grinned. "I do not recommend that you try copying my dear Rosalind's ways when you're with my brother," he said, looking at his betrothed with eyes that twinkled with merriment. "Timothy has been brought up to eventually be an earl, and he is a great deal more aware of his own self-importance than I shall ever be.''

"Oh, I should think that by the time you're the Prime Minister of England you'll have quite an air of consequence about you," Rosalind told him, chuckling. "I am sure I shall have the deuce of a time bringing you down to my level when you return home each evening."

"Rosalind," Judith scolded sharply. "If Mama heard you she'd wash out your mouth for using such language. What must Christopher think of you?"

"That deuce is a darned sight better than devil for a choice of words, I should think," her sister snapped. "And if you're going to run to her with tales of how Christopher and I argued over houses, we'll ask Peter to come with us in the future."

"It won't do any good," Judith said with a cheeky grin. "Mama says he doesn't stay close enough to you both. I tell her that I never leave you for a moment, but she doesn't realize that you sometimes leave me. But you know, I'm learning a great deal of what I should and should not do just by sitting and listening to the two of you."

"You'd best not use us as pattern cards, my dear Judith," Christopher admonished, "for we're not at all like the usual affianced couple, and neither of us has any desire to be used as an example. Whether it's Timothy, or any other gentleman you're with, just be yourself and you'll get along famously."

When they reached Upper Brook Street, they had to describe each of the houses they had looked at that day, and Lady Stockton seemed relieved by their description of the one they liked the best.

"Don't get anything too large to start with, my dears," she advised, "for there'll be time enough for that later, when you start with a family."

It was difficult to tell whether Rosalind's flushed cheeks were due to the idea of starting with a family, or to the realization that Christopher had been right about the houses. The glance they exchanged, however, gave her a strange feeling inside of both warmth and longing, and she could not help but wish there were just the two of them in the room at that moment.

He left shortly afterward, for he had been forced to neglect his duties these last few days, but had worked late in the evenings to catch up.

He had not been back in his office at Holland House for more than a half hour, however, when Georgina Walters opened the door and came in, carefully closing it behind her.

This was not at all the thing for a young woman to do. Had it not been for the fact that he wished to speak to her about the note he had received from Rosalind, Christopher would have opened the door at once. However, on this occasion he much preferred that no one else should hear what he meant to say to this strange relative of the Hollands.

"I'm glad to see you have returned," he said, coming straight to the point, "for I have been waiting to speak to you about a note that Miss Marshall gave you to deliver to me. Why did you not hand it to me in the normal way, instead of placing it upon my desk, and leaving me in the dark as to how it came to be there?"

"Oh, Chris," she said, summoning what she obviously thought was an understanding smile, and using a diminutive of his name that he and his family detested. "I realized that the girl had a tendre for you when they dined here that evening. And though I knew, of course, that you would not wish me to encourage her foolishness, she was so very persistent that I had no option but to bring her note back with me. I was anxious to get rid of it, though, and you were not in your room when I knocked on the door, so I went in and left in on the desk for you, without even thinking you would wonder where it came from."

"Rosalind tells me that the letter I received was not the one she wrote to me," he said grimly. "For what purpose did you rewrite it?"

She gave an incredulous little laugh, then asked scornfully, "Why should I do something like that? I don't know the girl in the slightest, but it was difficult for me to refuse to do her a favor when you and I live in the same house. If she says the letter is not the one she wrote, then she's not only foolish but a liar to boot.''

"It was not even written on the same stationery as she uses," he said, his expression one of complete disbelief, "but on a much inferior kind, and I checked when I came in that night and found that there is a supply of exactly the same quality paper in the downstairs study here.''

"I would never think of opening someone's letter unless it was addressed to me,'' she pronounced, "and as for the writing paper she used, it was a comparatively cheap kind that is available everywhere, including here at Holland House, as you say.''

He felt sorry for her, but even if she wouldn't admit to it, he had to make her realize he knew for a certainty that she was the culprit.

"We did not meet just this year,'' he told her, watching her expression closely. "We first met more than a year ago near Miss Marshall's home in the country.''

Just for a moment she looked startled, then she said, "I don't know what you're talking about, but has it not occurred to you that she may have made the whole thing up just to get your attention?''

"No, it has not occurred to me,'' he said grimly, "for she has always had my complete attention and affection since the day we found each other again. I must tell you that Miss Marshall and I are now betrothed. We mean to be married just as soon as this business with Napoleon is over and done with.''

"You've been taken for a fool,'' she cried, a look of horror on her face. "I'm sure it was all a trick to bring you up to scratch, and you allowed her to succeed. How do you think you're going to get out of it now?''

"But I have not the least intention of trying to get out of it, Georgina,'' Christopher said quietly but firmly. "I've loved her for a very long time, and can think of nothing I want more than to make her my wife.''

"I can see that you are completely infatuated with her. However, I know it to be a fact that I did nothing except take the letter from her and place it upon your desk," she said in a soft but most convincing tone of voice. "It does occur to me, though, that this whole incident may have been just a rather clever scheme to bring you up to scratch." She smiled wanly. "If so, then it has most decidedly served its purpose, hasn't it?"

His expression was scornful but his voice quiet as he said, "I must ask you to leave now, Georgina. This is my office and I have a great deal of work to catch up on. Please close the door behind you, and I hope that the next time we meet you will have come to your senses."

When she did not move, he rose and went over to the door, opening it wide and standing there waiting until she finally shrugged slightly and walked slowly out of the room. In the corridor she turned and gave him a triumphant little smile before going off in the direction of the stairs.

He sat at his desk for the better part of fifteen minutes, trying to think why a young woman with her education and opportunities would deliberately try to make mischief against someone she scarcely knew. To him it made little sense, but then he had never before had much to do with the working of female minds, or at least those of the *ton,* with the exception, of course, of his own mama, and she had always been very different.

There was a great deal of work awaiting his attention, however, and he was soon immersed so completely in it that he completely forgot all about Georgina and her decidedly distasteful insinuations.

It was a little after ten o'clock when Lord Holland came into his office to discuss some of the correspondence that had accumulated.

"How are you and that young lady of yours going along with finding somewhere to live?" he asked. "You know, of course, that we'd be glad to put a suite of rooms here at your disposal, but I have a feeling that you lovebirds would want a little more privacy than we can offer."

"It's most kind of you, my lord," Christopher told him,

grateful for the offer, "and Lady Holland already mentioned as much, but I believe that we have found something suitable today, only a short walk from here. We're going to look again tomorrow, but I have the strongest feeling that we'll take this one, for it would seem to suit our needs extremely well."

"You mean to rent a place before you marry, I suppose, so that it will be ready for you to move into immediately after the wedding?" Lord Holland suggested. "Save your money, though, and offer to take whatever house you decide upon from the date you want it, rather than from today. Get the agreement and everything signed, then you've no need to worry about losing it in the meantime. They'll jump at it, believe me, for there's little chance they'll get another tenant for it this far into the Season."

Christopher had always been aware of Lord Holland's practical nature, and appreciated the advice.

"You're right, sir, and I'll most certainly do that," he said. "The wedding will be in the country, and it is our hope that you and Lady Holland will be able to attend."

Lord Holland smiled. "By all means send us an invite, my boy, but I'll tell you now that there's little chance of our attending, for I don't get very far these days, as you know, and I'm sure that my lady wouldn't want to come on her own. You'll have our best wishes, though, for we both felt that Miss Marshall had a good head on her shoulders and that she'd make you an excellent wife." He chuckled. "And you know well enough that Lady Holland does not say that about many of the young society chits she sees these days."

Christopher was fully aware how vastly relieved Lady Stockton would be to know the Hollands would decline her invitation, but he still smiled and said, "Just the same, I'll make sure you get an invitation, sir, in case circumstances should make your attendance possible."

"You're still determined to join Wellington, are you?" Lord Holland asked, though it was obvious that he knew the answer.

"Yes, sir, though I know and appreciate your feelings on this subject," Christopher said grimly. "Despite the fact that you like the fellow, Napoleon must be stopped and put away somewhere that he can't escape from this time."

"You're probably right, though you'll never convince Lady Holland, of course," Lord Holland sighed. "He's a most interesting fellow, however, and it's sad to see a brain like his not put to better use. How long do you think it will be before you're off?"

Christopher shrugged. "It's hard to say. We're nearing the end of May now, and it could be a couple of weeks, or perhaps a month. But I've the strongest feeling that two weeks from now I'll be on my way to Brussels."

"You'll do what you have to do, I know," Lord Holland said, clasping Christopher's hand. "Just make sure you come back in one piece, my boy, that's all."

He left then, and Christopher watched until the door closed behind him before heaving a sigh. The Hollands had met Napoleon many years before, and formed a lasting friendship. And though Lord Holland still admired certain traits in the fallen emperor, he was completely against and denounced some of the crimes the man had committed. To Lady Holland, however, he was a hero, and with the permission of his jailers she had regularly sent newspapers to him while he was in captivity on Elba.

Chapter Fourteen

Rosalind was finding her days far more irksome than she had ever thought to when she had at first consented to marry Christopher. Although she knew that the constant presence of a chaperon was just as trying to him as it was to her, she began to feel that they would never be alone again until their wedding night. And sometimes, when he made little effort to get her to herself, she wondered if, perhaps, he no longer cared.

Lady Stockton, upon whom the burden of her daughter's displeasure inevitably fell, was trying hard to arrange a wedding with her hands completely tied by the bridegroom. At first she had thought they might be able to set a date and then, once the two were married, Christopher would forget this ridiculous idea of going back to war, for he would not wish to risk leaving Rosalind a widow.

In the last supposition she was quite correct, for he did not wish to leave her in such a position, and his solution was most definite. They would not marry until the whole situation with Napoleon was over and done with. But it had never occurred to him that his and Lady Stockton's ideas of a quiet wedding in the country might be so vastly at odds.

"I don't know how that young man thinks I can keep on making plans without setting a date," Lady Stockton moaned. "And now that we're dining with his mama this evening, it's even worse. What am I going to tell her about the wedding?''

"I wouldn't tease yourself at all about Lady Glastonbury if I were you, Mama," Rosalind said, being practical. "She brought him up, so surely she must know how terribly stubborn he can be. The village church does not see more than six weddings a year, so there'll be no problem there with whatever date is finally set. And after all the times I've been poked and prodded to make sure that my gown fits, it must surely be ready in time. It may, in fact, be yellowing with age before it is ever worn.

"My chief concern is in making definite arrangements about the house. It is my hope that he signed a lease today on the one we saw last week, for then I can begin to work upon it.''

"I thought that it needed no work," Lady Stockton said with a frown. "Surely you don't mean to spend a lot of money on a rented house?''

"Of course not," Rosalind told her, adding, "but the curtains in the master suite were dreadfully heavy and did not let in sufficient daylight. I only mean to take measurements of the windows and replace them with something lighter. But I cannot, of course, do so until he has actually signed the agreement on it.''

Her mama shrugged. "Well, I'm sure you know what you're doing, my dear," she said. "What will you wear this evening?''

"My pale blue lace, I believe," Rosalind said. "Though I've asked Hetty to press the lemon brocade as well, in case I should change my mind.''

Lady Stockton shook her head, for it was apparent that her daughter felt every bit as nervous about the whole situation as she herself did.

They need not have worried about the dinner at the Glastonburys, however, for it was a huge success. The two mothers got along extremely well with each other, and, of course, Judith and Timothy were by now good friends—if not a little more than that.

"I understand your problems completely," the countess said to Lady Stockton in the most sympathetic tones. "But we do very little these days in the way of socializing, so you need not worry about our being unavailable on any date you finally decide upon. We would, of course, cancel anything it conflicted with, for my son's marriage would take precedence even over a royal command.''

Lady Stockton was extremely gratified, and smiled, saying, "Well, we must certainly hope that it does not come to that, for I hear that the Prince Regent is very quick to take offense."

"I should think that, by then, he and almost everyone else will, at that time, be so busy celebrating our victory over Napoleon that no one will notice when we go off to the country for the wedding," Lady Glastonbury said, smiling more confidently than she felt, for just the very thought of Christopher going into battle again put her into a dreadful quake.

The ladies were alone, sipping tea in the drawing room while their husbands had retired to the earl's study to drink port and smoke a cigar.

A little to Lady Stockton's concern, which was in fact justified, the two brothers had taken Rosalind and Judith into the gardens for a stroll in the cool evening air, and as soon as they were out of sight the couples had drifted off in different directions.

"I'm so glad that you signed the lease on that house at last," Rosalind whispered, giving a little shiver of anticipation as she felt Christopher's arm slide across her back and draw them close together. "Now if only you would agree to procure a special license, we could get married quietly and then at least have a few days together before you have to go."

He looked down into her anxious face and slowly shook his head. "I would dearly love to do just what you suggest, my dear, but I cannot in all conscience agree to do so," he murmured. "If I were to be killed it would be bad enough leaving you a widow, but you would eventually marry again. However, were I to live but be severely wounded, you might find yourself with an extremely bitter, helpless cripple on your hands for the rest of your life."

"That's nonsense, for you could just as easily be injured

taking a fence," she argued, though she knew that it was useless
to do so. "At least I would have a perfect few days, perhaps
even a week, to remember."

He shook his head. "It's not enough. You deserve much more
than that, and I mean to see that you get it. So let's not have
any more talk of entirely ruining your mama's plans. If we were
to do such a thing, she'd not talk to either one of us for months,
and I, for one, would not blame her."

"You're right, of course," Rosalind said ruefully. "But if
I could only get you to agree, I would be willing to take my
chances with Mama. She gets very cross indeed when things
don't go as she planned, but I'm sure she would get over it
eventually."

"And what about the wedding trip I'm arranging?" he asked,
a secret smile playing at the corners of his mouth. "Would you
be willing to forgo that?"

"As you mean it to be a surprise and won't give me even
a hint as to where we're going, I don't know if I'd mind or
not," she declared. "And we could always take it afterward,
couldn't we?"

"Perhaps," he agreed, amused by her perseverance, but quite
decided on the matter, "but it wouldn't be quite the same, you
must admit."

He placed a finger beneath her chin then looked at her lovely,
trusting face. Infinitely slowly it seemed, his lips descended until
they touched hers at last, brushing them lightly at first, then
returning to capture and plunder until her head swam, though
every other sense seemed doubly alert. She clung to him, not
even knowing that she was instinctively returning his kiss, and
pressing herself closer to his strong, hard body—making his
decision all the more difficult to maintain.

The sound of a nearby giggle brought them back to the
present, and Christopher reluctantly released her, knowing as
he glimpsed the glazed expression in her eyes, that he had made
matters worse rather than improving them. There was now no
question in his mind that she desired him just as much as he

did her, though she, in her innocence, had not the least idea of what it was she longed for.

He heard his brother's cough and knew it for an advance warning, so that by the time the other couple appeared, he and Rosalind were simply holding hands, though their faces would have given them completely away had the moon been but a little brighter.

Judith looked somewhat chagrined, and Timothy slightly amused, as though the young girl had expected a great deal more from her first stroll with a gentleman in the moonlight.

"I believe that we'd best rejoin the ladies before they think to send a search party after us," Timothy said, still smiling, as he took Judith's hand and placed it upon his arm. "We could all do with a cup of tea, I believe, provided our mamas have left us some."

As they neared the French doors, the sisters hurried ahead but the two brothers lingered in the moonlight for a moment.

"I assume she did not succeed?" Timothy asked, smiling.

Christopher chuckled, shaking his head. "She has no idea, however, how hard it is for me to resist, but I'll not spoil the rest of her life for the sake of what is probably no more than a couple of weeks. It was so very tempting, though. Was Judith bribed to get you out of the way?"

"I really don't think she needed much bribing, for she's quite a little minx. And an interesting one, though she, too, was disappointed, I'm afraid. I do not make a habit of seducing young ladies in their first Season," Timothy told him, a regretful note in his voice.

"Nor in their second Season, I would hope, if the lady in question is shortly to be my sister-in-law," Christopher murmured, chuckling softly as he steered his brother through the door and into the drawing room. "Did you leave us any tea, Mama?" he asked.

"I just sent for some more, but I'm not at all sure that you deserve it," the countess said, a fond smile belying her words. "It's a wonder these young ladies didn't catch a chill, out in the garden for so long without so much as a wrap around their shoulders.''

"But it was not at all cold," Rosalind protested. "In fact, it was quite beautiful out there in the pale moonlight.''

The two older ladies exchanged glances of amusement tinged with envy, then the earl and Lord Stockton entered, the latter looking quite pleased with himself.

"A little more hot tea will be here shortly," the countess said. "Would either of you like a cup?''

The two men refused, but seemed happy to sit with them while the others sipped the fresh, warm brew and nibbled on cakes and pastries.

"Did I hear you say that you had settled upon a house, my boy?'' the earl asked his stepson.

"Yes, sir," Christopher said. "I believe that we were fortunate and would not have secured it were it not so late in the Season, for it was rented earlier and had to be abandoned when sickness broke out at home. Or at least that is what the agent said.''

"Do you have the keys yet, Christopher?" Rosalind asked. "I'd like to go there tomorrow and measure the windows of the master suite, for I do dislike the heavy curtains which are there, and must replace them before we move in.''

"I have the keys, but if you could wait a couple of days for me to get caught up on my work, I could go with you," he suggested, then smiled as she shook her head impatiently. "Very well, I'll send them around to you in the morning, but take a maid with you and just be careful that you don't fall.''

"Yes, 'Mama,' " Rosalind mocked, and he laughed and shook a fist at her.

"Oh, I'll come with you, Rosalind," Judith said quickly, "for I'd like to take another look at the place, and then I can also go along with you to pick out the new fabric. We'll take Hetty with us, of course, and if Mama is using the carriage we can always hire a hackney.''

"I don't at all like this habit you girls have started of riding around in hackneys," Lady Stockton said severely. "If Peter is not back in time to take you, why not wait until the afternoon, when the carriage will be available?''

She saw her hostess's amused smile and added, ''You can have no idea, Lady Glastonbury, how difficult it is to bring up girls in this day and age. They're always wanting to go off on their own somewhere, defying convention, and one hears of the most dreadful things happening. They simply cannot apprehend that there are rogues, pickpockets, cutpurses, and worse, all over London, just waiting to take advantage of young ladies like them.''

The countess's smile held a hint of sadness. ''I can fully understand how worrisome it must be, but I must say that though I am immensely proud of my fine boys, I still envy you your girls, and bless you for letting us take Rosalind into our hearts.''

Lady Stockton positively beamed with pride. ''She is a dear girl and is completely capable of running a household, for she has always been of considerable help to me both in London and in the country,'' she said, adding, ''and my dear Judith, in this her first Season, has seemed to grow up all at once. I do believe that having an older sister with her has been a considerable advantage.''

As the young people had now finished their tea, the Stocktons decided it was time for them to make their departure. They left then, with promises to keep in close touch as further plans for the wedding developed, and Rosalind was interested to note how her mama and papa had so quickly changed their minds about Christopher's eligibility. It seemed as though Lady Holland was now forgotten.

Christopher, who returned to Holland House late that evening, was at work in his office before eight o'clock the following morning, and had fortunately made considerable progress with the accumulation of correspondence when Georgina knocked on his door and put her head around.

''Good morning, early bird,'' she said brightly. ''Lord and Lady Holland would much appreciate your company at breakfast. They've missed you these last few days, as I have also.''

Before he could reply she was hurrying off down the corridor, so he put away some of the more important papers, locked his desk, and strolled off to the room at the front of the house where family breakfasts were always served.

It was a cheerful room, with a view of Kensington Gardens where, it seemed, there were always at least a few people taking an early stroll or a canter.

"Good morning, sir, my lady," he said, giving a polite inclination of his head, "and to you, too, Georgina, for you left so quickly you gave me little time to greet you."

"Good morning, my boy," Lord Holland said. "It's good to see you back. Just help yourself to whatever you fancy and don't skimp, for we've a lot of work to do today."

After serving himself with bacon, kidneys, poached eggs, and a generous helping of finnan haddie, Christopher took a seat at the table and reached for toast, butter, and coffee.

"I notice that you're not very hungry this morning," Georgina teased. "What a pity there was nothing to which you took a liking!"

He grinned. "It's a good thing you came to remind me, for I had become so immersed in the work which was pending that I had forgotten all about breakfast. But I'm sure I would have remembered eventually."

"How are Lord and Lady Glastonbury?" Lady Holland asked. "Well, I trust?"

"Very well indeed, my lady. My mama has become extremely fond of Rosalind, and is looking forward to having her for a first daughter-in-law. They had the Stocktons over to dinner last evening, and I am afraid that the mutual admiration became, at times, a little sickening," he told them, smiling ruefully, "but I suppose that it is better for both Rosalind and me if our respective parents stay on good terms."

"Much better," Lord Holland grunted. "Stockton has always seemed to me to be a very sensible, practical sort of fellow."

"He would appear to be blessed with sound common sense,

but I cannot say as much for his wife," Lady Holland remarked. "She was a bit Friday-faced, I thought, looking down her nose as though nothing here suited her."

"Perhaps she had second thoughts about accepting the invitation," Georgina said slyly, "but felt unable to cancel at the last minute."

Lady Holland shrugged as if she did not care one way or the other, then said, smiling, "We'll leave you to finish your breakfasts, for it looks to me as though Christopher hasn't eaten for a week. Will you be in for luncheon, my lord?"

"I think so, my dear," Lord Holland responded, then, as the two women left the room, leaving the door open a crack, he turned back to his protégé.

"I didn't want to say anything in front of Lady Holland, but it looks as though it won't be long now before Napoleon will have a considerable force behind him. Have you any idea how prepared Wellington is?" he asked.

"A great deal better than he was a few weeks ago," Christopher told him. "Then there were no more than ten thousand British troops and a few Hanoverian units. I now understand that there are about twenty-five thousand, with more going over daily. There'll be more Hanoverian forces and Dutch-Belgian coming along as well, but most of those will, I'm afraid, be untrained troops. As you probably guessed, sir, I came back today to straighten things out here, and will probably leave for Brussels within a week."

Lord Holland nodded thoughtfully. "You know, if you've not settled on a house you like as yet, my offer is open. Lady Holland and I would still be glad to let the pair of you have an apartment here at Holland House. We've plenty of room to spare. You could use it for just as long as you wished, and it would save all this last-minute searching."

"That's very kind of you, sir," Christopher said, smiling gratefully at the older man, "but as a matter of fact we have found a most suitable house not much more than a fifteen minute walk from here. I decided not to wait, but to sign a lease on it and, actually, Rosalind and her sister are going over there this morning to take measurements for new curtains, or something of the sort.''

"Which direction is it?" Holland asked.

"It's on the north side of Knightsbridge, sir. It's the last house on the very first row of houses to the west of the Life Guards Barracks. It's not very large, but there's ample room for the two of us to start with," Christopher asserted.

"I would think so, my boy, and it's always a very wise thing to start small. The walk back and forth will be good for you after being cooped up here all day," Lord Holland said. He looked across at the door, which was slightly ajar. "It seems the ladies forgot to close the door. Would you mind doing so, Christopher, for I want to tell you about an incident in the House that is for your ears only."

As he neared the door, Christopher heard the rustle of skirts, but thought nothing of it at the time, for he was curious about the incident Lord Holland had mentioned, and anxious to hear what he had to tell him.

A short time later they went into the older man's study to take care of some bills and correspondence, then Christopher returned to his own office.

He was surprised when Georgina knocked and came right in a few minutes later, but when she behaved as though they had never had harsh words, he decided to let the matter rest for now.

"It must be very exciting to be a man and know that you are shortly going to make history," she told him, her eyes alight with a look of almost longing. "Females never get to do anything exciting."

"Yet they make history every day," Christopher said, dryly. "And I don't believe that any sane individual would willingly choose to go to war."

"But surely that's exactly what you are doing?" she suggested, appearing not to apprehend his meaning.

"We fight for our ideals, I'm afraid," he said rather ruefully. "Patriotism, freedom for our children. Though there's a decided feeling of comradeship in a regiment, the men who truly enjoy going into battle are usually the paid mercenaries—men who will fight on either side just for the fun of it.''

"I see what you mean," Georgina returned. "I suppose I was not really thinking of the actual battles, but just being in the army with a lot of other men.''

He nodded, and hoped that she had something to do this morning away from the house, for he had a long day ahead of him and he could not get started while she hung around. Yet he had no wish to be rude to her unless she brought up the matter of the letter again.

But she had no intention of staying in today, and had only wanted to make quite sure that he had so much work to do that there was no chance of his leaving Holland House for quite some time.

"I'll go now and let you get on with your work. But if you're not at the luncheon table today, I'll come back and remind you, for you must keep up your strength, you know," she said in so odd a tone that he glanced up sharply. But she had her back to him and did not even turn around when she reached the door, closing it quickly behind her.

With a sigh of relief, he reached for the papers he had locked away before going in to breakfast, and was soon immersed in the problem of turning them into a summary form for Lord Holland to read.

Chapter Fifteen

When Hetty came into the bedchamber to help her mistress dress, Rosalind thought, at first glance, that the abigail had been crying, then she realized that the poor girl had caught a most dreadful cold.

"You must tell Cook that I said you were to be given a hot posset and sent back to bed at once," she ordered, her sympathetic smile belying her seemingly stern words, "for neither my sister nor I wish to catch that dreadful-sounding cold. Nor do we want the rest of the household in bed with it. I'll come by and make sure that you obeyed me, for we want you up and about as soon as possible."

Once the girl had hurried from the chamber, Rosalind picked out the muslin gown she meant to wear that day, and took it with her to her sister's chamber.

"Get up, sleepyhead," she called softly. "I'm going to help you dress this morning, and then you can fasten my gown for me. Hetty's sick, so I've sent her back to bed."

Judith yawned and stretched lazily. "Oh dear, I don't know what I'm going to wear this morning yet," she said, "it's too early."

"Well, you'll recall that you're coming to the house with me to help measure the windows in my bedchamber for new curtains, so I'm sure you'll not want to put on anything too fancy.''

Mornings were not Judith's best time of day, for though she did not waken bad tempered as a rule, it always took a long time before she was truly alert.

"Well, if you're wearing your green muslin gown, I suppose I should wear my old blue one," she muttered, blinking. "What hour is it? It surely cannot be time to get up as yet."

"It's nine o'clock, and I want to be at the house we've rented by a half past ten," Rosalind told her as she stepped into her own gown. She presented her back to her sister. "Come along and fasten me up. It will help you waken, I believe."

Judith's fingers were more awake than the rest of her, for she deftly fastened her sister's gown, and, yawning once more, she stepped away from the bed, then took a close look at herself in the pier mirror. Frowning, as though dissatisfied with what she saw, she went over to where Rosalind had poured some water into a bowl.

"Come along," her sister said, handing her a washcloth. "The cool water on your face will do wonders for your complexion."

"Will it really? I've never heard of that before," Judith muttered, then thoroughly splashed her face, blinking as some of the water went in her eyes.

It took a quarter of an hour before she was completely presentable, and then, with eyes wide open at last, she reached for a brush and comb to attend to Rosalind's hair, for it was even more unruly than usual.

"We were so late home last night," Judith said, a mischievous smile on her face, "that our mama may decide to have her breakfast in bed, and we can be out of the house and in a hackney before she realizes that Hetty is ailing this morning, and not with us. Do you have something to measure with?"

"Yes, I've already put some tape into my reticule. Let's go down at once, and have breakfast while the food is still hot," Rosalind urged, "and before anyone else comes down to ask where we're going."

Even though they went down at once, the meal was a more hurried affair than usual, and then there was a slight delay until one of the footmen was able to find the key that Christopher had sent over, just fifteen minutes before. After Rosalind had placed the weighty key in her reticule, they slipped out of the house and walked quickly to the stand and stepped into a hackney.

Once they were on their way, Judith turned to her sister and remarked, sniffing daintily, "I don't know what it is that makes a hackney so appealing, for the smell is simply dreadful and I'd not be at all surprised if our gowns are stained with dirt and grease when we step down."

Rosalind chuckled. "It's probably because our mama dislikes them so. You know, forbidden fruit or something," she said. "It's also very much easier than sending for a carriage and waiting for it to come around, then watching our old coachman put on that terribly disapproving expression of his because we do not have a maid with us."

When they reached the house, Rosalind stepped down quickly, then reached a hand up to help her sister.

She produced the heavy key and inserted it into the keyhole and, to her surprise, it turned quite smoothly with almost no effort at all. Then she put it back into her purse as they stepped inside.

"Let's take a walk around each floor once more before measuring that window," Judith said eagerly. "It's such a pretty house inside—except, of course, for those curtains which you're quite right about—and I think you were so very fortunate to find something as nice as this."

"It was Christopher who found it, for he always seems to know just where to go and what to ask for. And he's so pleasant with the people he has to deal with that they willingly bend over backwards to help him."

"Doesn't it worry you that he means to join Wellington quite shortly now?" Judith asked, serious for a moment. "I don't think I could bear it if Timothy meant to go over there."

"Of course it worries me," Rosalind told her, so softly that her voice was no louder than a whisper. "But it also makes me very proud of him. Can you understand what I mean?"

"Of course," her sister said, nodding. They were both sitting on the top step of the third flight of stairs, and she jumped up, saying, "Come along and let's get those windows measured, or we'll not have time to go to the fabric shop before luncheon."

She started toward the bedchamber, with Rosalind close behind, and once inside they went over to the wndows immediately. Rosalind produced the piece of tape and a measuring stick, and then pulled a chair closer, for her to step on first, before climbing onto a large chest directly beneath the window. She held the tape to the top left corner, and then let the other end drop so that her sister could put it against the window ledge. Judith carefully measured the tape and made a notation.

"That's the length," Rosalind said. "Now we'll see what the width is."

So intent were they in making sure the measurements were correct, that they did not hear the door to the hall being quietly closed and locked. They did, however, hear something that made them glance around, and then came the sound of the key being turned in the door that led to the master bedchamber. They both ran over to it at once, but found that the heavy door did not yield in the slightest—and neither did the door to the hall.

Rosalind turned to her sister, frowning. "Why would anyone want to lock us in here?" she asked, completely puzzled. "I suppose I should have locked the front door behind us, for it must be someone playing a rather foolish practical joke, but there's nothing much we can do now. Mama knows where we are, and will surely send someone around to look for us when we're not back for luncheon."

"It's more likely to be the middle of the afternoon before someone comes, I'm afraid," Judith said ruefully, "for we've both made so much of a habit of being late for luncheon that she'll not worry about us at first."

"It's a pity that we don't have a couple of decks of cards with us, for we could both use some practice at piquet."

Rosalind said practically, and went over to the chest of drawers she had been standing on. But though she searched completely through it, she found neither cards nor anything else that might help pass the time.

She glanced out the window, and saw the back view of a cloaked figure walking along the street and something about the woman's carriage and the way she held her head seemed vaguely familiar. But try as she might, she could not quite recall who it reminded her of.

Judith was looking through some old fashion magazines she had found in a bookcase, and Rosalind went over to join her, picking one up and leafing through it to pass the time.

They had been locked in the chamber at least ten minutes when Rosalind started to sniff something, and then they looked at each other in horror.

"It's smoke that I can smell," Rosalind declared, though still finding it difficult to believe. "It's not a practical joker at all, but someone meaning to harm us. We've got to get out of here. Let's try to get one of these windows open. I didn't know why I put a screwdriver in my reticule when I took the measuring tape this morning, but now I'm glad I did."

"We can't jump," Judith said, her voice rising in alarm as she looked down below.

"Of course, we can't," her sister said calmly, "but there are linens on the bed and more on the daybed in the dressing room. Start pulling them off while I work on the window, for it seems to be a little stiff."

"Look, Rosalind. The smoke is coming under the doors, we're going to be trapped here," Judith said, now very close to hysteria.

"Oh no, we're not, and don't you dare think it for a moment," Rosalind told her, a great deal more confidently than she did, in fact, feel. "The window is quite loose now, but I don't want to open it until we're ready to get out, for it may draw the fire and smoke inside. Now, you take hold of the opposite corner of this sheet and we'll twist it to make a rope, then we'll do the same with the others and tie them together."

There were more sheets on a shelf in the dressing room, and these received the same treatment, then Rosalind tied one end of the makeshift rope to one of the legs of the heavy chest in front of the window, using a knot her brother had taught her years ago.

Judith had started to cough as more and more smoke came into the chamber, but she stopped when Rosalind pushed up the heavy window and fresh air entered the chamber.

"Can't you go first and then help me?" Judith asked, pitifully, but Rosalind shook her head.

"No, I must see you safely down first. I know you can do it. Just twist your foot around the rope, and then lower your hands one at a time until you're almost crouching. Then take your foot out and twist it in again a little lower. You're very nimble and you'll soon get the hang of it. Don't look down, and you'll be all right."

It was such a pity, Rosalind thought, that she was the only one who had been brought up with Peter, for he had taught her a great many things young ladies did not, as a rule, get a chance to learn, like tying knots and climbing ropes.

Judith was out of the window and moving slowly down when a gentleman suddenly appeared below, seemingly from out of nowhere, and Rosalind watched while he reached out and helped her sister down the last few yards. Now it was her turn.

"Catch!" she called, as she threw first Judith's reticule and then her own out the window. Then, giving the makeshift rope a sharp tug to be sure it was still secure, she started down, and though her skirts hampered her progress, it was not long before a strong arm came around her and brought her safely to the ground.

"My name is Jeffries, and I believe I have met you once before," the gentleman who had so ably helped them said. "It was at a dinner at the Hollands, if I'm not mistaken."

Rosalind remembered him, but had too much on her mind to do more than nod.

"I have a carriage nearby, my ladies," Lord Jeffries went on, "and though I have no idea why you are both climbing out of a window, I would be only too glad to take you home."

"Because there is a fire in the house. Cannot you see the smoke starting to come out of the window I just left?" Rosalind asked him. "We must go back inside and see if we can put it out, and then find out how much damage has been done. You see, we are renting this house, and we—oh, dear, it all sounds so complicated that I'm sure you must believe by now that we set the fire ourselves."

She hurried to the front door and flung it open, but though the smell of smoke was strong, she could see no sign of any fire in the downstairs rooms.

As she went upstairs, however, it became warmer and the smell more distasteful, for flames were starting to creep along the lovely wood floor. Oil-soaked rags had been piled in front of both entrances to what was to be Rosalind's bedchamber, and it was these that had been set alight, but had, it seemed, caused more smoke, until now, than actual fire damage.

"Let's each take up a bucket of water from the kitchen," she suggested to their would-be rescuer, "for we must stop it spreading any further."

It was not until after Rosalind and Jeffries came down with their empty buckets, and went to refill them, that Judith stirred herself, then, giving her sister a weak smile, she made for the kitchen to do her share. The fires were soon out and the surrounding wood soaked down well to prevent them starting again, but the smell was less easy to get rid of.

Rosalind flung wide all the windows and doors to let out the unpleasant odor, then, after disposing of the burned rags behind the house, she sat for a moment on the bottom step of the stairs. She was not so much concerned about the house, for the actual damage was fortunately very little, but she felt sure that had she and Judith remained in that smoke-filled bedchamber for long, they could conceivably have died. Though they had got out fairly quickly, her chest felt quite sore, and Judith could not yet stop herself coughing every few minutes.

When she saw Christopher coming toward her from the direction of the kitchens, Rosalind stared at him as though she did not know who he was, for she had not the slightest idea that he was in the house.

He crouched down in front of her, thinking how adorable she looked with soot on her nose and cheeks, and her hair in such disarray that he was forced to wonder if it might ever be the same again.

"Your mama is outside," he said softly. "And I've been talking to Jeffries, and it seems that you're the heroine of the day. Have you any idea what happened?"

She looked at him steadily for a moment, then said quietly, "Yes. I believe that someone tried to kill us, or at least to seriously harm us. We were measuring the window in what will be my bedchamber, when someone locked first the door to the hall, and then the one to your chamber. I hadn't noticed, but I suppose that keys had been left in all the doors by the agent.

"Rags must then have been piled outside each door and set on fire. Please don't tell me that I am imagining things, for the evidence is right here."

"I know, for I saw the rags and they could not have got there by accident. You say someone actually locked the doors to your bedchamber. Did you hear them do it?" he asked, finding it almost unbelievable.

She nodded. "At least, we must have heard something, for we turned at the same time, and saw that the door to the hall was closed, and then we quite distinctly heard the key turn in the door to your chamber. We thought at first that it was a prankster, and meant to wait until someone came to look for us, but when we smelled the smoke we climbed out through the window. Lord Jeffries came inside with us and he can tell you exactly the way we found it."

"I believe you, my dear," Christopher said. "I don't have to ask him. Have you any idea who could have done such a thing? Did you happen to see anyone?"

"I looked out the window and saw someone walking west who looked rather familiar. But you wouldn't believe me if I told you who I thought it was," she said a little sadly, for just a moment ago she had recalled who it had looked like. "So it's best that I hold my tongue until I am more certain of the facts."

"I might believe you. Try me," he suggested, an expression of such tenderness in his eyes that for a moment she was almost persuaded to do so. When she shook her head he asked, "Who knew that you were coming here this morning?"

"You, Mama and Papa, and our abigail, but she was not at all well this morning so I sent her back to her bed," she replied. "It's always possible that some of the other servants knew, of course, and Peter may have known also, though I didn't see him to tell him our plans."

"You can add at least one more, for I told Lord Holland that you would probably be here today," he said, "but I cannot conceive of his having any connection with it."

"Of course not," Rosalind agreed, smiling faintly.

Christopher's eyes narrowed as he suddenly remembered closing the door to Lord Holland's study, and hearing the rustle of a gown as he did so.

"How did you and Mama come to be here at this time?" Rosalind had just realized that neither he nor Lady Stockton could have known they were in trouble.

"By the most incredible stroke of luck, I would say, for I had to run an errand in town, and as I was looking for a hackney to return to Holland House, your mama came along in her carriage and offered to take me up.

"She suggested stopping here in case you had not yet left, though I told her I thought that by now you would have gone to look for materials, and that you had my key," he said. "We found the front door wide open to let out some of the smell. Judith is with her now."

"I suppose I had better go out to her, to let her see for herself that I'm all right," she said, taking the hand he was offering to help her rise. "I'm afraid your bedchamber and the hall are in an awful mess from both the fire and the water we used to put it out."

"Don't worry about that for a moment. I'll have the estate agent send someone here to take care of it. Did you complete your measuring?" he asked, smiling a little grimly.

"Oh, yes, for at first we didn't worry too much, thinking it was someone playing a practical joke—that is, until we started to smell the smoke," she said softly. "I still find it difficult to believe that anyone would do such a thing."

"Was the person you saw a man or a woman?" he asked, looking at her closely as she considered her reply.

"A woman, in a wine-colored cloak," she told him.

"Was she wearing a hat?" he asked.

Rosalind nodded. "Yes, she was wearing a bonnet a shade lighter than the cloak—and now I recall seeing light gray ribbons fluttering from it."

"One more question, and then we'll go out to see your mama," he said. "Can you recall what Georgina Walters wore on the occasion that you gave her the note?"

"On the day I gave her the note we met to have ices at Gunter's, and she had on a blue pelisse and a matching bonnet," she said, "and the day before, when Peter and I saw her and I suggested meeting the next day, she was wearing a green bombazine carriage dress and a matching bonnet with lighter green feathers. Why do you think it might have been her that I had seen? She's not one of my friends, but I do not bear her any malice, even though she did change the letter to you."

He frowned. "I'd rather not say right now, and must ask you not to say anything either until I am sure. Did you mention any of this to Judith?"

"No, you're the only one I've told and I'll say nothing at all if you think it best," she told him. "But if it was her she ought not to get away with it."

"I promise that she won't," he told her. "But I'll find out for sure when I get back. I know she went out this morning without telling anyone, for the errand I had to run was one of her duties, and I went because she was nowhere to be found."

"You know, she could have been just walking along the street, Christopher, and only have been passing this house, for it's not very far from Holland House.'' Rosalind was trying hard not to accuse the woman out of hand.

''She could,'' he admitted, ''and I've had quite a bit of experience at interrogating people, so I'll be very careful as to how I phrase my questions. And now I think I'd best take you out to your mama. I'm quite amazed that she has not come looking to see what we're doing in here alone.''

Rosalind's impish grin surfaced for a moment. ''She probably has enough on her hands with my sister, for she was terribly frightened, you know, and I had to be a little harsh to make her go down the rope.''

''You did only what you had to do, I am sure,'' Christopher assured her. ''For if you had not acted as you did, Jeffries would not have seen anything untoward happening, and your mama and I might have arrived too late, for the two of you could have suffocated in that bedchamber, you know.''

''That was what I was afraid of,'' Rosalind admitted, ''for Judith was coughing a great deal, long before I was able to get her to climb down.''

They went outside then, and when Lady Stockton had finished hugging her older daughter and thanking Lord Jeffries, she took them up in her carriage and they went directly home.

Christopher, having declined to accompany them, also refused Lord Jeffries' offer of a ride, for as he walked the mile to Holland House he wanted time to think, to plan carefully, and then decide how best to approach the problem of making Georgina Walters incriminate herself.

He had wondered if she might not be a little mentally disturbed after she had forged that letter, for the things she had said to him had not sounded rational.

The first thing to do, of course, would be to find an opportunity to look through her armoire, preferably while she was not in the house. He decided that the most satisfying way would be to have her return the favor he had done her this morning. She could run an errand for him this very afternoon.

His step was eager as he entered Holland House, but when the butler informed him that the others had just gone into luncheon he made sure that Georgina was with them, and decided that this would be a better time to make the search. On the pretext of washing his hands, he hurried upstairs.

The door to her bedchamber was not locked and he quickly slipped inside. To his surprise, the first thing he saw, laid across the bed, was a wine-colored cloak. The bonnet that had been tossed onto the bed was a slightly lighter shade, and the brim was lined inside with light gray, the exact shade of the ribbons that tied it on.

Opening the door to the armoire, which contained only a dozen garments, he saw both the green bombazine dress and the blue pelisse.

He picked up the gloves from the bed and noticed a distinct smell of petroleum. A closer examination showed that three of the fingers were scorched. Slipping them into a pocket, he hurried downstairs.

"We did not wait for you, Christopher, for you know full well how I feel about anyone who comes late to the table," Lady Holland said severely.

"I do indeed, and offer my profound apologies, my lady," Christopher said, giving her a charming smile. "My thanks also for your kindness in not insisting I eat in the kitchen, as my mama used to do when I came late to table."

"Not since you grew to be such a handsome charmer, I'll be bound," Lady Holland said, chuckling, and quite forgiving his tardiness.

When they had finished, Lady Holland left the dining room first, as usual, but Christopher placed a detaining hand on Georgina's arm.

"If you can spare a moment, sir," he said to Lord Holland, "I would like a word with you and Georgina, in your study."

The older man looked surprised, then said, "Of course, my boy, you two go inside and I'll be with you as soon as my old bones will let me."

Keeping his hand on Georgina's arm, Christopher walked ahead, but as they reached the door she tried to free herself.

"If you don't mind," she said, "I must just go upstairs for a moment."

Christopher shook his head. "Later," he said sternly and she gave him an angry glance, before going into the study.

Once he was settled comfortably behind his desk, Lord Holland looked at Christopher and said, "I had thought you meant to talk about your departure for Brussels, but now it appears to me that you have a more pressing problem."

"Yes, sir," Christopher said. "I'd like to ask Georgina some questions in your presence."

"Go ahead, my boy," the older man said.

Christopher placed himself carefully between the door and Georgina's chair. Then he asked her, "Where were you this morning when we were looking for you to perform an errand for Lord and Lady Holland?"

"I had to go into the city. No doubt Lady Holland forgot that she had asked me to do so," she said haughtily, "but I don't know what concern it can be of yours."

"Lady Holland did not send you anywhere, Georgina, and I would suggest that you did not go near the city at all. Instead, I believe that you went to the house that I have rented in Knightsbridge. Isn't that true?" he asked sternly.

"You must be mad," she replied scornfully. "Why should I go anywhere near there?"

"You went because you had overheard me telling Lord Holland exactly where it was, and that Miss Marshall and her sister would be there this morning," he told her, then he reached inside his jacket and pulled out the gloves.

"I just took these from Georgina's bedroom, my lord. Smell them, and take a look at the burns on the fingers," he suggested, then grabbed Georgina's arm as she tried to snatch them off the desk. He then pushed her quite roughly back into her chair.

"She was seen there wearing the cloak and bonnet that are now on her bed, and will no doubt also smell of petroleum and be a little charred," Christopher told his employer, adding, "While the two young ladies were measuring the windows, it seems that someone locked both the doors to the bedchamber they were in, placed oil-soaked cloths in front of them, and set them on fire.''

"It wasn't me," Georgina said wildly. "I didn't go near the house and if anyone says I did they're lying. It must be someone who knows what sort of a person that young woman is and decided to make her pay for it."

"Do you remember asking me to close the door this morning, sir? When I did, I heard the rustle of skirts, and I had just told you about the house we had rented and exactly where it was," Christopher said to Lord Holland.

Then he turned back to the girl and started to question her in the way in which he had interrogated French prisoners, and it was not long before Georgina broke down completely and admitted to what she had done.

"I'll deal with her," Lord Holland said, shaking his head grimly, "and I give you my word that she'll never have the chance to harm anyone again."

Chapter Sixteen

When Christopher called on Rosalind the following morning, she knew at once that he was leaving for Brussels very soon, for there was a remoteness in his eyes, as though a part of him was already over there.

"How long have we left before you go?" she asked him softly.

"How could you possibly know?" he asked, puzzled. "I've only just received word myself, and I came here directly to tell you."

"It's written here, and here," she said, touching her fingers to the corners of his mouth and the sides of his forehead, where faint lines had appeared that were not there before, "and also in your eyes. They tell me very clearly that you must go, and that you'll not be happy again until it's over."

"I have to leave in two days' time," he said softly, "and I know that the waiting will be dreadful for you, but we'll not talk of that just now. Let us at least enjoy the short time we have left together. Will you come for a drive with me this afternoon, just the two of us in Timothy's curricle? He's lending it to me until I go. Should I ask your mama?"

"She can have no objection to our riding in an open carriage," Rosalind said, "for I was permitted to do so with Timothy before I even knew he was your brother."

"His title made a lot of difference to your mama, and then, of course, you were not betrothed," he said wryly.

"Just come," Rosalind said firmly, "and I'll make sure that Mama agrees."

He nodded, inestimably pleased at her determination. "I have to go now, for there is much to do, but I'll be back at two o'clock to take you up." He reached for her hand and lifted it to his lips. "Till then, my love," he murmured, then turned on his heel and left.

Lady Stockton was not home, for she had taken Judith for a fitting of a new gown, and when they returned for luncheon Rosalind told them of Christopher's visit.

"You saw him in here alone?" her mama asked, eyebrows raising at such an indiscretion.

"What was I to do, send him away?" she asked angrily, then remembered that she must obtain permission for their ride in the park. "We want to drive in the park this afternoon, Mama, just the two of us, and his purpose in calling was to ask your permission."

"You know very well that you cannot drive with him in a closed carriage, Rosalind, so why did you not tell him so?" Lady Stockton asked, a little more kindly than before.

"Because we will not be in a closed carriage," Rosalind explained. "Timothy has loaned him his curricle until he leaves, for he has, of course, a great many things to do in just two days."

Lady Stockton smiled and nodded her head. "How very kind of Timothy, and, of course, you may ride in an open carriage. I trust you, however, not to do anything that would cause people to talk."

"Oh, Mama," Rosalind said, sounding exasperated. "When have I ever done something like that?"

"Was your first meeting in Rutland at all proper?" Lady Stockton asked pointedly, "and then did you not meet him with just a maid in attendance in Kensington Gardens?"

Rosalind had, at least, the grace to blush. "I assure you we will sit the correct distance apart, and we will not hold hands,

I promise," she said quite demurely, then spoiled the effect with a mischievous grin.

Lady Stockton shook her head in exasperation as Rosalind ran from the room to go and change for the drive. She meant to put on one of her loveliest new gowns, one that Christopher had not yet seen, and she would wear with it a matching bonnet and parasol.

"Poor Mama," she said to him when he had arrived at last and was handing her up into the curricle. "She'll be most relieved, I should imagine, when we are married and she no longer has to watch me so very carefully. I must tell you that when I asked her permission she carefully pointed out to me the most improper way we met on the first two occasions."

He looked puzzled. "The first time was a little improper, I must agree, but the second . . . ?" He raised an eyebrow.

"It was when I just happened to be strolling almost in front of Holland House, with just a maid," she told him.

He grinned. "She has a point, I'm afraid, but you'll not be such a problem to her for very much longer now."

Something inside of her seemed to do a little jump just at the idea of what he had said, but she dare not cross her fingers in case he should realize how frightened she was that he might be killed or wounded. Instead, she gazed at him, but that was even worse, for then her whole insides began to feel weak. If he had the slightest inkling of what she meant to do, she knew that he would be furious with her.

"And will I be a problem to you, do you think?" she asked him daringly.

"I've no doubts about it," he told her with a grin. "But I'm completely sure that you will be worth all the trouble."

"I hope you will always think that," she murmured, a mischievous gleam in her eyes.

"I'll not guarantee it, for there are sure to be times when I could cheerfully wring your little neck," he told her, laughing now, "but then there will also be occasions when you will want to do me some dreadful harm. Our marriage will never be dull, I am certain, but it will never be lacking in love on either side."

Rosalind's cheeks turned a bright pink, and she swallowed hard as she looked into his eyes and saw in them the emotions not quite hidden in their depths. It was the greatest consolation to know that he loved her just as much as she loved him.

He turned his head as a friend on horseback, Lord Sutton, who Rosalind knew only slightly, hailed him. They spoke for a few minutes about the journey to Brussels, for they were apparently traveling there together, and Rosalind's ears pricked up as they arranged to meet, with their horses, at the London docks, cross to Ostend where they would spend the night, and travel the next day from there to Brussels.

"Is it a lengthy crossing to Belgium?" she asked when the friend had ridden away.

Christopher shook his head. "It's only a matter of a few hours, but it can be most uncomfortable if the channel happens to be rough," he told her, grinning at her expression of distaste. "And the journey to Brussels is not quite as far as from London to Rutland. We will get an early start and do it in a day, but ladies would, of course, make an overnight stay."

She frowned. "Will there be ladies there when the battle commences?" she asked.

He shook his head. "By now I should think that most of the ladies who went over there, with their dandified gentlemen, for the parties and the excitement that sometimes precede a battle of this sort, will be on their way home, fleeing like rats deserting a sinking ship," he said dryly. "And it's a good thing, for their sort would only be in the way when the fighting really begins. There are always some women, however, wives of officers and enlisted men, who help with the nursing, of course, and they do an excellent job."

He placed his hand over hers and squeezed gently. "I'm sorry Sutton and I ran into each other like that," he told her tenderly, "for I don't want you to be thinking about it and worrying. No matter what anyone tells you, you must not expect to see me as soon as you read that it's all over. There'll be much to do afterward, and I don't want you imagining all kinds of terrible things."

"I won't," she promised, trying hard not to reveal what she meant to do.

"Oh, look, there are Judith and Timothy, and Mama is with them," she said, somewhat surprised.

"She's probably keeping an eye on us," he remarked with a grin. "Just sit up straight and pretend that we're the merest of acquaintances—and I'll try to do the same."

There was no reason for them to stop and talk as they passed each other, but they smiled and waved politely in the completely accepted way, and when they were out of earshot Rosalind could not help letting a tiny giggle escape.

Two days later, Christopher left for Brussels, after dining the night before with the Stocktons. His brother was also present at the dinner, and afterward the two couples walked in the garden, separating when they could no longer be seen from the house, so that Rosalind and Christopher could have a little privacy.

If Lord and Lady Stockton noticed that Rosalind looked as though she'd been kissed when they returned, no one made any comment, not even the next day.

Now Rosalind could go out with just a maid accompanying her, and she took advantage of this at once, going first to the house that would be her home very soon now, and making an inspection of the work that had been done to repair the damaged floors and the bottoms of the two doors.

At luncheon she deliberately affected a dejected expression, and did not enter into the conversation as she normally would. Eventually Lady Stockton commented on it and gave Rosalind just the opportunity she needed.

"Why don't you go to see Nanny Giles for a day or two?" she suggested. "I can't go with you, for with so much going on right now I must be here to keep an eye on Judith, but you could take Hetty with you. It's a pity that Peter went off to the races for a few days, but Nanny will bring you right out of yourself, I'm sure."

Not by even so much as a blink of an eyelid did Rosalind

give herself away, though she could not believe in her good fortune. They could leave about ten in the morning, in a hired chaise, and Rosalind had no doubt that the driver would be only too happy to take them to the docks instead of to Maidstone if she gave him the larger fare.

Fortunately, money was not a problem, for she rarely spent more than half of her most generous quarterly allowance, and Lord Stockton had just given her the allowance for the third quarter. In case something should come up, however, she would also take a few small pieces of jewelry with her to sell if necessary. To allay their worries if anyone started to wonder about the length of her stay with Nanny, she would leave a letter in her writing case, saying where she had gone, for this was the most likely place her mama would look, should she be concerned.

The next morning, the two of them left, and Rosalind had not been out in her guess that the driver would much prefer to drive them to the London docks than to Maidstone. He chuckled to himself as he pocketed the money, but Rosalind was careful not to go near any of the boats until he had driven his carriage away.

"Where are we going, Miss Rosalind?" Hetty asked in a worried voice. "This isn't the way to old Nanny Giles's place."

Rosalind ignored her for a moment while she looked around, and then saw some soldiers boarding a vessel. Taking the girl's arm, she hurried over and made inquiries of one of the young soldiers.

"Yes, miss, this is the one for Ostend, and if you're going aboard, you'll need a ticket from over there," he said, pointing to one of the sheds.

"We're going to Brussels, Hetty," she said to the girl, adding, "or at least I am, but I'll not force you to go if you don't wish to come with me."

"And leave you alone with all them men, miss? Cook would flay me alive if ever I did such a thing. I don't like it, but know it's no good trying to stop you, once you've made up your mind," the girl said, picking up the small traveling bag and following her mistress.

With tickets in hand they headed back to the boat on which the soldiers were standing, then, making sure once more that it really was the right vessel, they stepped aboard.

Rosalind stood at the rail, as far away from the dock as she could in case anyone should recognize her and spread the word in town.

Hetty stayed as close to her mistress as possible, as if afraid that one of the men might grab her and assault her where she stood, but none of them seemed at all inclined to do anything of the sort.

"I'll be glad when it sails," Rosalind said, "for I'll not feel this is real until we've left the docks behind. I'm sorry to surprise you like this, Hetty, but I couldn't ask you to come with me, and expect you to say nothing to Mama."

"I'd not have told on you, Miss Rosalind," the girl said, giving her mistress a look of admiration. "I don't say you're doing the right thing, but I wouldn't have given you away. Does Mr. Ferguson know you're doing this?"

Rosalind shook her head. "I simply couldn't keep on going to balls and parties as if he was just over there on some sort of a spree. And if he should be wounded, I mean to take care of him, no matter what he says."

She stopped speaking then, for a hooter was sounding so loudly that she couldn't hear her own voice, and then the gangplank was drawn up. The boat lurched awkwardly at first, before moving away from the dock and toward the middle of the river.

There was the sound of a throat being cleared behind them and Rosalind turned to find the young man she had spoken to on the dock, trying to get her attention.

"There is a cabin below, ma'am, that you might find more comfortable if it should get a bit rough," he said to her.

"Thank you, but I was told that I'd be much less likely to be ill if I but stayed on deck," Rosalind said, though she was grateful for his suggestion. "Perhaps I will see if I can remain here for a little while longer at least."

"Yes, ma'am, but if you do decide to go, let me know, for you might need a strong arm to help you down to it. I'll be just over there," he said, pointing to a spot where several young men were sitting on coils of rope.

"I will indeed," she said softly. "You're very kind."

The crossing proved to be quite calm, however, and she was able to stay on deck for the whole journey, but they disembarked into a town that was in complete turmoil.

Passengers for England were trying to get aboard the minute the gangplank was let down, for there were far more people waiting for the boat than it could ever take.

To Rosalind's surprise, the soldiers formed a wedge with the ladies in the middle, and thus they were able to disembark without being pushed overboard by the press of people. The inns were all full, however, and when the young man found them a carriage to take them to Brussels, both women were grateful and, in fact, they slept most of the way there.

With so many trying to leave the country, there was little difficulty in securing accommodations in the town, and Rosalind was able to get two rooms that overlooked the main street. One had a little veranda, but she dared not go out onto it for fear of being seen and recognized.

"What are you going to do now, Miss Rosalind?" Hetty asked.

"I'm going to wait here until all the soldiers leave, I suppose," Rosalind said. "Can you go down and see what food you can find? Anything will do, for I'm not really very hungry."

Hetty came back fifteen minutes later with a loaf of bread, butter, eggs, a piece of ham, and a jug of milk, and Rosalind surprised herself by the way she thoroughly enjoyed the simple meal.

"Did you hear anything of interest?" she asked the girl when they had both eaten their fill.

Hetty nodded. "They say that the soldiers will be leaving soon for a place called Quatre Bras. We'll be able to see them as they march down the street,'' she told her mistress.

They sat waiting, not saying very much, and soon there came the tramp of boots as the soldiers marched off to battle. Rosalind sat near the window watching, not daring to go onto the balcony to cheer them along as others were doing, including Hetty who stood out there, waving to them as they passed.

Then Rosalind saw Christopher, and tears came into her eyes. He was riding a black horse, and he looked magnificent in his scarlet jacket trimmed with blue and gold. She stepped back as he passed on the other side of the road, for she did not want him to see her. The last thing he needed at this moment was to worry about her presence there.

All night long, soldiers marched down the street, some no more than young boys, who had no idea what they were going to see the next day. Others were old, with faces grim and scarred from previous battles. They did know what lay ahead, but they went just the same, for much the same reasons that Christopher had gone. And finally, the street was quiet once more, and the whole town seemed to be sitting there, listening.

The waiting was intolerable. It would have been, no matter where Rosalind was. Then the first reports came through, to the effect that Napoleon had been victorious, and suddenly the streets were once more alive with people leaving for Ostend as fast as they could go, and offering ridiculous sums of money for the most uncomfortable forms of transportation.

''What do you mean to do, Miss Rosalind?'' Hetty asked as they looked upon the tumult down below.

''I'm not leaving until I know what happened to Mr. Ferguson,'' Rosalind said firmly, hoping desperately that she was making the right decision.

Then word came that the armies had met again at the village of Waterloo, and that this time Wellington had been victorious and the French army completely routed.

Rumors about the number of dead and wounded seemed surely be be grossly exaggerated until the injured men began to straggle into town, some staggering painfully along, while others were carried by their comrades.

Praying that Christopher had been one of the more fortunate ones, Rosalind now hurried downstairs and, for the next few days, she and Hetty joined the women who were already doing whatever they could to ease the pain of the men, until the tireless surgeons could get to them.

As she walked past a row of severely wounded boys lying on stretchers, she heard a faint call, "It's the lady on the boat," and she turned around to see the young soldier who had been so helpful to her on the crossing and at Ostend, but he had the look upon his face that she had come to dread.

Crouching down beside him, she said softly, "It's my turn to help you now. How can I make you comfortable?"

"Write a letter to my girl," he whispered. "Her address is in my pocket. Tell her I tried my best to get back to her."

She took his hand in hers. "Try just a little harder and I'll not need to write at all, for you'll see her yourself," she said gently, but then his hand went limp in hers and his head sank forward.

The surgeon crouched down at the other side, then shook his head. "He's gone, I'm afraid, ma'am," he said, and called, "orderly."

"Let me just get his girl's address from his pocket," Rosalind said as an orderly came forward. "And I need to know his name." The orderly waited until she had taken the scrap of paper from the boy's pocket, then one of the other patients said, "His name is Private Jim Wagstaff, miss."

Scarcely realizing what she was doing, she wrote down the name and slipped it into the pocket of her apron, feeling a terrible sadness for the girl she had to write to.

He was not the first, and by no means the last, of the many men and boys Rosalind tended who would never see England again, but she learned to look after the living also, for the less severely wounded needed careful nursing to put them back on the road to recovery. Though the days of waiting for news of Christopher, who she asked for each time a new batch of wounded came in, were taking their toll upon her, she set to with a will, doing more work than she had ever done before in her life.

She was busy changing dressings and feeding men unable to help themselves, when Christopher entered the house where she was working. He was looking for men of his own regiment, and as his gaze went across the length of the ballroom, now converted into a hospital ward, he saw her, but thought at first that he must surely be dreaming.

She glanced up, as though he had somehow willed her to do so, and she met his unsmiling gaze with a look of pure disbelief. Then she turned back to the soldier whose dressing she was changing, quite obviously thinking that she had begun to hallucinate.

Then one of the soldiers called across the room, " 'Ere, Colonel. You lookin' for us?''

He went over and spoke to the men, and one of them, who had seen the direction of his glance, said, ''She's a beauty isn't she, sir? But it's no good looking at her, for she says she's taken.''

He turned to gaze at her steadily for a moment, but this time she was concentrating on fastening a dressing in place, and did not see him.

''She'd better say so, if she knows what is good for her,'' Christopher told the soldier.

He sat talking quietly to his men then, but watching Rosalind all the time out of the corner of his eye, and noting with surprise how efficient she had become at harder work than he had thought her capable of.

When she had done everything she could for the last of the soldiers, on the opposite side of the room, she rose and started to walk across the floor toward him, too tired to even realize that she was not hallucinating. Then he got up and went to meet her, slowly at first—and then they were both hurrying, hungry to be in each other's arms.

Their kiss was long and sweet, despite the cheers of the men enjoying the scene and shouting their encouragement. When he finally realized they had an audience, Christopher drew apart somewhat, but did not relax his hold upon her.

"I think we'd best find a more suitable place than this to talk, don't you?" Rosalind suggested.

"To talk?" he asked grimly. "It's not talking I feel like doing to you right now. How could Lord and Lady Stockton allow you to come here and be exposed to all this?"

"They didn't," she admitted cheerfully. "I came without telling them, and now I'm glad that I did, for most of the visitors from England left as soon as they thought they were in danger."

"Come along," he said, pulling her in the direction of the door, but Rosalind shook her head.

"I can't," she told him. "Someone has to relieve me before I can leave here, but it will be Hetty, and she won't be more than a few minutes, I know."

"Who's Hetty?" he asked.

"My maid, of course," she told him. "You surely don't think that I would have come here alone, do you?"

"I'll be damned if I know what you'd do, at this point," he said, shaking his head in bewilderment, "but I know what I'm going to do next."

She looked at him curiously.

"I'm going to find a padre and make an honest woman of you right away, before your father has a chance to get his hands on you," he told her.

When Hetty came hurrying in to relieve Miss Rosalind, she could hardly believe her eyes, for she had quite given up hope of ever finding Mr. Ferguson, although she knew that her young mistress had not. But the look of happiness on Miss Rosalind's face was unmistakable.

Chapter Seventeen

There were padres to be found, quite a number of them in fact, but neither Rosalind nor Christopher had the heart to try and pull them away from their infinitely more important task of comforting the severely wounded men.

As they paused before crossing the main street, Christopher looked more closely at Rosalind and saw for the first time the lines of weariness on her face and its total lack of color.

"How long have you been on duty?" he asked her. "You look as if you are completely worn to a thread."

"Only eight hours," she said quietly, "but it is more emotionally exhausting some days than others, and this was one of the bad ones. You must not worry about me, though, for I'm perfectly well, and will be fine just as soon as I've had some rest. I've not been sleeping well of late, but now that I know you're all right, I know that I'll sleep better tonight."

They had reached the door leading up to the rooms where Rosalind and Hetty had stayed since their arrival.

"You mustn't come up, not because I'm at all worried about people talking, for they have much more to do here than waste time in idle gossip. But the stairs are steep and they will hurt your leg," she said shortly.

It was clear that there was nothing further he could do for her at the moment, so he pressed a tender kiss upon her

213

forehead, and left her to make her way up the stairs to her rooms. Then he went in search of one more man who he knew had been wounded, and must find before he left Brussels.

Major Robert Horton was the friend of Peter's, who had once saved Rosalind from her mama's wrath in their dimly-lit garden. He had since become a good friend of Christopher's as they had spent long, wearying hours together planning strategy and had then, later, put it into action.

They had been fighting side by side at Waterloo, and had Horton not stepped in when Christopher was being attacked from behind, he would not be here now. But Christopher had then seen Horton go down, and there had only been time enough for him to make sure the wound was not life-threatening, before he was himself beset on his other side by a couple of French officers. When he had looked for Horton once more, his friend had been nowhere in sight.

But by now Christopher was very tired, for the old leg wound had opened up again during the fighting, and having neglected it for the last several days, he knew that he needed to have it attended to very shortly if it was not to continue giving him trouble.

As he entered yet another of the large houses being used to nurse the wounded, he stood, for a moment, looking around, then realized he could scan the room just as easily from the comfort of a nearby couch. As he eased himself down, however, a familiar voice hailed him.

"Christopher, old comrade, glad to see you came through in one piece."

He jumped up at once, and his leg almost gave way at the sudden movement, then he carefully made his way over to where Robert Horton sat on the side of a cot, his left arm in a sling.

"I don't know how I missed you, Robert," he said as he drew nearer, "for you're the man I was looking for. Do you think you're in good enough shape to stand up for me at my wedding tomorrow?"

Horton looked puzzled. "Surely you're not deserting Rosalind for someone you've just met out here, my friend? Think on it carefully before you do anything so rash, for it's hard to undo once the knot is tied.''

Christopher smiled a little grimly. "It's Rosalind that I'm marrying. Can you believe that I left her in London and found her here today tending the wounded? Her family must be sorely worried as to where she is, and I think it best that we wed before returning to England, else she'll be hopelessly compromised.''

A sly smile spread slowly over Horton's face. "It would not be the first time she's been compromised, nor perhaps the last. I'd be willing to wager that you never saw her in sleeping cap, night rail, and dressing gown, as I once did.''

"What's that you say?" Christopher thundered, jumping to his feet, but spoiling the effect as his leg gave way once more, and he sat down again more quickly than he intended.

Horton put up his good right arm to protect his grinning face.

"It was in the presence of her brother and another gentleman, of course, and I'm sure she must be hoping I've forgotten about it long ago. You see it was like this," he began, and proceeded to tell his friend what had taken place at that inn on the London road.

As the tale came to an end, Christopher chuckled, shaking his head in wonderment, yet not truly surprised. "You have to admit that she's quite unique," he said, adding a little ruefully, "and I do not anticipate many truly dull moments for years to come, but I'd not wish it to be any other way. I need you tomorrow to convince the padre that we are already affianced, for he might otherwise refuse to marry us at such short notice.''

"And there I thought you were seeking me out only to offer your assistance in my time of need," Robert Horton said, chuckling a little. "And, by the way, it would appear to me that you could use a little medical help also. It would seem to me that you sustained an injury to your leg.''

Christopher shook his head. "It's merely an old wound that is giving me a little trouble," he told him, then turned as he saw that his friend was beckoning one of the surgeons over.

"Let's see what old sawbones here thinks about it," Horton suggested, and before Christopher realized what was happening, the surgeon and his assistant had swung him onto the cot and were carefully taking off his boots.

"Now, Colonel," the surgeon grunted, over Christopher's protests, "you know better than to leave something like this unattended."

He spent a rather painful quarter of an hour, but when they had finished, he had to admit that the leg was a sight more comfortable, and would be even more so, he was sure, after a good night's rest.

"Would you happen to know where the padres are billeted?" Horton asked the surgeon before he left.

"They're across the street at number fifty-seven when they're not busy giving comfort to the wounded," he said, "but I wouldn't have thought either one of you would be looking for their ministrations."

"The Colonel here wishes to get married in the morning," Horton told him.

The surgeon looked dubiously at Christopher. "I must say that I'm surprised, Colonel, for you don't look like the kind of man who rushes his fences. Who is the young lady?"

"You may have met her," Horton said, as Christopher glared fiercely at him. "She's Miss Rosalind Marshall, and I can assure you that they are already affianced, for I saw the notice in the *Gazette* some weeks ago."

"Allow me to congratulate you, sir," the surgeon said to Christopher, now most earnest, "for she's one of the finest young women I've met. But I'm surprised indeed that you permitted a young lady of quality to come over here at a time like this."

"That is why we need to marry at once," Christopher explained, "for I was completely unaware of her intention of coming to Brussels, and I found out that she was here but a few hours ago."

"Ah, now I understand your predicament, Colonel," the surgeon assured him, "and I'll personally see to it that one of the padres attends on you as soon as possible."

He was as good as his word, and a young chaplain appeared not a half hour later, more than eager to perform a happier service than he had grown accustomed to during the last sennight. It was arranged that the two officers would bring the bride to him early the next afternoon.

Word of the wedding spread quickly throughout the town, however, and by the time Rosalind awoke and started to get ready for her next nursing shift, she found that someone else was taking it over, and that she was to have the kind of marriage service her fellow nurses felt she deserved. A Belgian matron, who was also helping with the nursing, had produced her own white gown and veil, and a large parlor had been set aside for the ceremony, which was to be attended by as many as could fit in the room.

There would have to be a second wedding, Rosalind felt sure, for her mama would insist. But no matter how much trouble Lady Stockton went to, nor how many guests of quality were to attend, it could never compare, in her own estimation, with the warmth and affection that surrounded her in this room today.

"Dearly beloved, we are assembleld here in the presence of God . . ." the chaplain began, and some minutes later, as Christopher placed a hastily procured ring upon her finger, she could not help but think of his beautiful rings that she had left at home for fear they might get lost or stolen on the journey.

" . . . whom therefore God hath joined together, let no man put asunder," the chaplain pronounced, and then she was in the arms of her husband, being very thoroughly kissed.

There was even a small reception afterward, with hastily prepared delicacies, and a cake waiting to be cut so that the health of the bride and groom might be toasted in a delicious local wine. As one group of friends left, another came in, for they had all grown very close during the time they had been together, and everyone was anxious to take part in such a happy occasion.

But it was finally over, and Rosalind escaped to change from the lovely gown into the dark green carriage dress and bonnet that she had come over here in, both of which had been miraculously cleaned and ironed so that they looked like new.

Christopher had declared that she should rest for a day before starting out for Ostend, and an innkeeper had set aside for them his best suite of rooms.

"You're still limping," Rosalind said as they walked toward the inn. "You weren't wounded and said nothing to me about it, were you?"

Christopher shook his head. "No, it's just the old wound that's been giving me a little trouble. It will be all right in no time once I can give it a bit of rest," he told her. "I hope you didn't mind all the fuss, but once we tried to find a padre it seemed that everyone found out our intention and wanted to share in our happiness. Enjoy it while you can, though, for once we see your mama and papa I hardly think they'll be pleased with either one of us."

"I can't blame them," Rosalind said, "for by now they must know that I did not go to see my old nanny, and never for a moment meant to. It's a good thing that we got married, or I do believe Papa might have carried out his recent threat to give me a thrashing."

"Are you trying to tell me that the only reason you married me was in order to get out of a thrashing?" Christopher teased.

She smiled. "There were one or two other reasons," she said softly. "I believe that, when all this is over and we're an old married couple, I'd like to come back to Brussels again. Will you bring me?"

"Of course," he readily agreed. "Did you have any special purpose in mind?"

She nodded. "Brussels will always have a very special place in my heart. You see, it's where I really grew up, I think. I had not the least idea, of course, what I was getting into when

I left London. All I knew was that I wanted to be there with you if you should be wounded and needed me. Then, when that awful rumor came that Napoleon had won, I was very frightened, but I just couldn't leave until I found you again.''

"You should have left, for it wasn't just a rumor," he told her quite sternly. "I'm afraid that it was quite true, for we did lose the battle at Quatre Bras, and there was a time when we very nearly lost at Waterloo, also, for we were severely outnumbered. You see, Blucher's forces didn't join us until seven o'clock in the evening, six hours later than they were supposed to. The heavy rains had delayed them.

"It's a good thing I did not know you were over here, or it would most definitely have affected my actions, for I'm sure I would have been constantly worrying about you.''

"I know," Rosalind said. "That's why I kept back from the window when you rode past. You didn't look up, but I was afraid that you might.''

He reached for her hand.

"If you ever do anything as dangerous as that again, I promise you I'll thrash you myself, though I've never in my life raised my hand in anger to a woman," he said, lifting her hand to his lips.

They had entered the inn and were relaxing in the comfortable sitting room of the suite, watching some noisy sparrows outside hunting for any morsel of food they could find.

"It's good to see them come back," Rosalind remarked, "for they all disappeared once the battles started. I suppose the constant sound of the guns scared them away.''

He nodded. "Speaking of battles," he said, "you're not really worried about what your mama and papa will have to say when we return, are you?''

"Not Mama," Rosalind admitted, "for she would grumble no matter what I did, but I do feel concerned about having caused Papa to worry so much about me.''

Christopher grinned. "He'll probably feel vastly relieved that his difficult daughter," he began, "has changed . . .''

" . . . into an eminently agreeable wife," Rosalind said, her eyes dancing, "as long as we both want the same thing."

"Oh, I think we probably do, or will do very shortly, I am sure," he murmured, as he gathered her into his arms and carried her into the bedchamber.